My Angel

A STORY OF SALVATION AND LOVE

A NOVEL BY

TETIANA BROOKS

Publication Consultants
Since 1978

ISBN 978-1-59433-474-0
eISBN 978-1-59433-475-7
Library of Congress Catalog Card Number: 2014907409

Manufactured in the United States of America.

Acknowledgements

I express my grattitude to my translator, Elena Zacharenko, editor, Rebecca Goodrich, and book designer, Jody Masty.

Being drawn into earthly passions,
I knew that, in going from gloom to light,
Dressed in black, Dark Angel
Would rush to shout: "Salvation is a lie!"
Yet, unassuming and lighthearted,
Delightful as a noble deed,
Afterward comes White Angel,
To whisper that hope is true indeed.

B. Okudzhava, 1924

Introduction

For My Dear Readers, With Kind Regards from the Author

All of my novels are based on the fates of real people. Any resemblance to the names and lives of actual people is purely coincidental, and all locations mentioned are used in a fictional manner.

I sincerely hope that the fates of my heroines will help someone out of despair, and to find the answers to life's seemingly insoluble questions.

I dedicate *My Angel*, my first book in English, to my beloved son Sergey. For her children a woman is ready to overcome any difficulty. Children imbue our lives with light, color, and meaning. Sergey has inspired my life with meaning. (He has also had bad luck, and maybe one day I will write about it.)

Neither this book, nor any of my others would have ever been written, nor would have seen the light of day if it hadn't been for my friends. To them I owe the fact that I had the heart to start writing, and if they hadn't supported me in this endeavor, then, of course, I couldn't have managed this by myself. I am grateful to them from the bottom of my heart.

The first thank-you I devote to my friend Irina Remezova. She was the one to convince me that the people I met along my way would be wonderful material for books. That the stories of life can help someone to find faith and a way out of the messes we all the time get into. Therefore there is something to tell and to share with the reader. It seemed that I never would, because it was one thing to talk, and quite another to write it so that it would be interesting to the reader. (Not to mention publishing the book, which wouldn't have happened if it were not for Irina.)

For the book design I am grateful to my longtime friend, a gifted artist and a wonderful woman, Natalia Korolyova. Natasha understood everything I wanted to express in this book, s no one else could.

The first editor and admirer of my talent was Alyona Madosik. We had to wander thousands of miles from our homeland to distant Alaska to finally meet. *My Angel* was written here in Alaska; I rolled the dice and entrusted it to Alyona.

Thank you, my dear husband, for doing your best to give me the courage to start writing. Thank you for having faith in me, and helping. You are one of the dearest people in my life. Without you and your support, this book would have never been created.

And now, dear readers, a few words for you. I truly hope you will enjoy *My Angel*, and the characters in my book. If they somehow help you to find a way out of a difficult situation, I will be doubly satisfied.

And now, good luck. God be with you.

Part One

Chapter One

For many years I'd been having the same night dream.

I come into a medieval town late in the evening or at night. The city is always empty. The street is illuminated with flaming lanterns, real fire flaring inside the white ball-shaped domes. I'm standing at the intersection of three streets, which form the letter Y.

A big, beautiful house of gray stone overlooks the streets, forming the upper part of the letter, and I always come down the tail of the street. I do not know the name of this city, or even the name of the street, but it always attracts and excites me. Every time I manage to get here, I walk through the deserted medieval streets and contemplate the houses, trying to understand where I am.

This dream is exactly how I imagine the medieval houses of wealthy citizens of that time. Pavement, buildings, walls, fences, everything is made of heavy gray stone, or from time-stained wood. Massive lanterns of wrought iron with ball-shaped domes with flames lighting the streets.

It's a bit scary, yet I am even more curious to know why there is not a living soul on the street. After all, in any city, even in the dead of night, you can meet a belated passerby. Someone may be coming back home from a vacation or a business trip, or after wetting his or her whistle on a friend's birthday.

And what about the lovebirds? They can be noticed in any city. *Noticed* is the best word here because they do not want to be stared at, but no matter how much they strive for intimacy they always get caught. When I go out at night this is what I see: Here's a couple kissing behind a tree in a park. And here's another one removing the light bulb in the entrance hall looking for a place to get cozy. That couple is simply walking around the city, holding hands and looking around amused, not recognizing their home-town. It seems completely unknown to them, so fabulous and beautiful is the power of love. Such nighttime lovebirds can be seen in any city. In any, but not in this one.

And what about the windows? I like to peep into the windows late in the evening. Someone in that room has a very beautiful chandelier. And the curtains in that window are amazing! I have to get the same for myself, just not claret-colored with silver but dark green with golden threads. Mostly warm green and other sunny hues predominate in my house. The palette of life.

And here are people sitting in the kitchen. Surely they are having a sociable drink. Nemiroff vodka with pepper, or Khortytsia, the platinum. Maybe some old friends scattered to the four winds have finally reunited. Or perhaps a neighbor simply dropped in to swig a glass before sleep.

In that window a young mother is carrying a baby in her arms. She is looking at him with eyes full of love and with a happy smile. Who will her beloved baby become, what kind of person will he be? Maybe he will become a world-renowned doctor who will save hundreds of lives and find a way to cure cancer. Or maybe he will end up as just a teacher at a school, but, certainly, the kind of teacher the children will love. Or maybe his destiny is to be a talented artist.

But in this city all the windows are so tightly shuttered that even a small gleam of light can't fight through them. Is it so late that everyone is asleep?

It was only once that I came to this town in the afternoon. It was warm and sunny. A lot of people in bright clothes crowded around. I came to my intersection in the usual way. I had two Russian sighthounds, Borzoi, on a leash: a female, Onega, that once lived with me and passed away, and a black male dog. I used to have a male Borzoi too, Leader, but he was white. He died with Onega, and their death was one of the biggest losses for me. Partly, it was my fault, and I always felt that.

But when I entered the city, my mood was sunny like the weather and the light all around. I was glad to finally see the people living in this city. I'd finally ask them the name of the city and would be able to just talk to someone. But everyone was so busy with their own affairs that day that no one paid me any attention. I would just have to come back, in another time of dream.

But I was never able to dream my way back again.

It would have been better never to arrive there in the afternoon. Because after I had left the city, I never came back.

But I know for sure when I come here again, it will be the same wonderful weather, but it will be the last dream of my life.

In the meantime, I was made to start my life anew.

I was only thirty-nine.

Truly, God works in mysterious ways.

Chapter Two

If you are married, you should always be prepared for troubles, large and small, insignificant and significant. I got tired of these disappointments and decided to finish his marathon of endless lies.

"So, where were you this time?"

"Well, my boss had lights down in his country house. I had to go to repair the electricity "

"Oh, there are no other electricians at the plant?"

"Everyone went home already. Why are you asking?"

"So you were the only one who didn't leave? Why was that?"

And so on and so forth. This went on for a long time. It was hard to believe that after sixteen years of seemingly happy married life such things could happen. I really couldn't remember how long this lie lasted, because I never had a habit of lying and trusted every word of my husband Aleksei.

But recently I began to notice that my good relationship with my son was somehow changing for the worse. He became irritable with me and frequently replied to me with a disdainful smile and dismissive words. That was if he replied at all. At first, as usual, I was thinking it was the awkward age that would pass soon. But with time more and more often I could hear, "You are so-and-so, yelling at me, making me do all these chores, while Aunt Marina..."

I became tired of hearing how wonderful Aunt Marina was. Whoever she was.

In 1991, the Soviet Union, the "Inviolable union of independent republics," collapsed. Ukraine became an independent state. As a result, everything created before was destroyed, while nothing was built to replace that. Not even offered. Enterprises turned bankrupt or were just closed so it was incredibly hard to find any job. Those who were lucky enough not to lose one had to manage without salaries as no one was planning to pay them for some time.

Six months later, when the backdated salaries were paid, inflation had grown by 300 percent or even more. Everyone survived as best they could; many people abandoned the city to develop little plots of food crops, and to get away from the noise and dust. One could have fresh tomatoes, dill, and parsley there any time, or could even start growing flowers, just for the beauty.

We decided to enjoy village life as were so many others.

So now we were sitting in the courtyard, surrounded by flowers, shaded by apple and pear trees. Watching how my hubby was plying a good knife and fork while we were having our usual conversation, I kept thinking, Do you really think you are the first one to try to get away with this? Do you think you are smarter than everyone else? From time immemorial men have been lying to women, all giving the same excuses, and it has never occurred to them that there is no need to say anything. Looking at this guy, who, to put it mildly, did not sleep at home, everything became obvious: twinkling eyes, avoiding looking at me, and this facial expression of a tomcat, who had just loaded up with cream or done something even worse for a decent man but so usual for a tomcat.

"So," I said. "If you really need this Marina, go! *Adieu*! But don't take my son there."

"Oh, so you're still going to tell me what to do!"

It is a well-known fact: attack is the best form of defense. Oh my gosh, I was so tired of all this! I had to find out who Marina was to objectively evaluate the situation. Though I'm an active and emotional person, I'm also a Virgo, and therefore had some common sense. I preferred to draw conclusions after having at least some basic information.

So. Who was he calling much lately?

Ira Romanova? No way. We had lost contact with her and her husband Sasha a long time ago. I wonder why? Somehow our paths diverged. It was a pity. I truly missed Irina. It would be so good to find her, find out how she was doing. And how was her daughter Karina doing?

Okay, this was not the main event now. Who could this other woman be? That's what I had to think about now.

There had to be someone who knew at least something about her, he had to talk of it to someone, to grumble and to discuss what a wonderful woman Marina was and what a bitch I turned out to be. Without a shoulder to cry on and to huff and puff about unfair fate, everything lost its meaning for my husband.

Ah! I knew! Raia Eremina. He was working with her in the laboratory. It had to be her. She must know something. It had become a habit for him to call her, her but not her husband Igor, which would be more logical. Which was what he used to do. The time had come to act!

"Raia? Hi, honey, how are you?"

"Oh, Polina, hello! Do not even ask. I almost broke up with Igor."

She was telling me the issues right from the start.

"Well, almost does not count. What happened? Look, this isn't a phone conversation. Pop by and we can chat, go over all of it."

"I would love to. Okay, tomorrow night, at five, I will be there."

"I will be waiting."

Raisa was a blonde woman with a nice body. She had large gray eyes, and was always using black eyeliner to show them off. In my opinion, a little too much eyeliner, but Raisa became extremely offended if you tried to give her advice about putting on make-up. So I was used to keeping my mouth shut.

Well, imperfect make-up was not the most important of Raia's disadvantages. The eyeliner was, as always, a bit too much, but I totally didn't care today. I put on my diplomatically sweet facial expression and I was ready to meet her, faking my pleasure to see her:

"Raisa! Hi, honey! Haven't seen you for ages! I've missed you incredibly." Forgive me for my insincerity, I prayed. "Come in. Come to the kitchen at once! You must be hungry."

The kitchen is absolutely irreplaceable for these kinds of chats. You can use it almost like a torture chamber, while it looks the exact opposite of one. People are ready to tell you much more than they have ever planned to.

"A glass of something?"

After the third vodka, the ice had been broken and Raisa began to complain, "Imagine, Polina, my Igor became jealous of your Aleksei. Big deal, so he took a few nice pictures of me, but it doesn't mean anything. Well, now we talk on the phone a little more often than usual, but we do work together."

Is there not enough time to talk at work? I seethed inwardly, but in the kitchen, I just kept refilling her glass. There is old Ukrainian wisdom that warns, "Say nothing to your girlfriend."

But Raisa was either not familiar with Ukrainian folklore or because my kitchen and vodka began to do their job, went on. "Well, we can't discuss our private affairs at work. And anyway, it's not about me. All of this is about Marina. How to help Marina."

Raia must have gotten completely confused as to whom to drink with and what to say.

"Can you imagine, her husband left her when their daughter was born six years ago, and just up and moved to Israel. The poor woman has been alone for so many years, not a single man in six years. And then she met Aleksei. His wife is such a—Oh! Polina, I am so sorry. This is another Aleksei, not yours, and I have to go now."

Raisa tried to stand up, but I pushed her shoulder to seat her back down, softly but surely. "*Shhh*. Stay!"

I pulled myself together. Relying on my pedagogical and psychological education, I cautiously continued, "Keep cool, Raisa! We have been friends for so many years. All men cheat. Generally speaking, I don't care anymore, but I feel so sorry for my son Vova. He's only fourteen, and can't understand everything; his whole life could go awry. Let's have one more glass for our friendship, for real women's friendship."

Raisa, knowing my, to say the least, extremely emotional nature, was looking at me like a rabbit looks at a boa constrictor, and I continued to dissemble.

"You know, I don't want anything from him anymore. If Marina needs him, I am ready to let him go. Clearly, though, it's going to be hard to be a single mom. All I need is just to talk to her. On the phone."

Raisa was speechless. Her mouth was hanging open.

"Well, let's have another glass for our kids, for their happiness."

It's almost a sin not to drink for that.

"Raisa, all you need to do is just give me the phone number. I will not tell anyone that you have given it to me. I will just talk to her. You also have a daughter. I am sure you want her to be happy. All men are bastards, and there's nothing more valuable in this case than women's solidarity."

I had no idea where such thoughts arose from, maybe even not thoughts but just words. In my head I was smearing Raisa over the wall with my anger and it finally seemed that she read all of this in my eyes. She slowly took the offered pen and paper, and wrote a phone number down.

I said to myself it better be the right phone number, or I'll do to you exactly what you are thinking I will do to you.

Some friend. Female solidarity. And to say nothing to your girlfriend, not a word. I *would* kill her. As soon as I was done with Marina.

Chapter Three

The phone number turned out to be correct.

I'd noticed a long time ago that if I wanted something badly, I always got it. At first I thought it was just coincidence, but now, after everything that has happened, I know for certain: we create our own destiny. By ourselves—our thoughts, our decisions, our actions. And beyond that, there is something that I don't fully understand yet, but I certainly know I have it. Whether it is some kind of force, or energy, well, call it whatever you like, but I know for sure—it is there. Now I have to figure out what exactly that is.

I think that you would agree with me. But we'll take that up again later.

Now I was pretty surprised that the phone number was correct. So pretending to be an employee of the telephone company, who had to verify a list of subscribers, I made a call and with a casually businesslike tone said, "It's the Subscriber Service Center of the ATS. Just verifying your subscription. Your last name?"

"Shalimova."

"Address?"

"Don't you have it?" She spoke with a hesitant voice. I knew she would offer no resistance.

"Look, I'm too busy to chit-chat, 'cause I have to ring up more than two thousand numbers. We regularly update all the info of our subscribers. Would you be so kind as give me your address," I continued to push.

"Two Kononov Street, apartment number seven."

Done. I couldn't force myself to continue. Oh! It took so much effort to fight with myself! And what for? It is a well-known fact: if a man wants to go, you will never make him stay. But why didn't he leave? Why was he running back and forth? What made that woman better than me?

I walked over to the mirror and saw a woman, nice in all respects. A slender, athletic figure. After all, I was a master of sport in artistic gymnastics in the past. Long, beautiful legs and full breasts, a cute face with expressive brown eyes and generous sexy lips. I always wore reasonable makeup, correctly emphasizing my femininity.

I knew I was not a top fashion model, but each time I passed a company of men, I was sure to hear compliments in my wake. Once Aleksei's boss said, "There exist very beautiful women. One glance, and you can't stop feasting your eyes on her! And then, there is a type of woman, who seems not to be a beauty, but you want her and you want her now!"

He was talking about me. Then why the heck was my dearest not satisfied? What must this Marina be like to make him barter me away, such a wonderful woman and the mother of his son? A Hollywood star or something?

Then the pain, insult, and loneliness overwhelmed me so that I burst into miserable, bitter tears. Letting all the sorrow free, it dawned on me: there's no use crying over spilt milk. Something had to be done.

Again I thought of Ira Romanova, a wise woman. When we were young, twenty-two or something, she once said, "For me the most important thing is that, once home, my Sasha leaves everything behind and is all mine. And I don't care what he does outside, without me; it's his business as long as he is happy." Clearly it was a self-sacrificing love that she had. Perhaps that was how it should be. I wondered how she was doing. I really hoped that everything was okay.

I would finish this epic soap opera, see it to the end, save my family and for sure I would try to reach her at some point. We would laugh at all this later. But I couldn't be like her. Jealousy was burning in me like fire, searing out all other thoughts. It deprived me of sleep and the ability to live normally.

So I pulled myself together and approached the mirror. Make-up should be flawless, hair and clothes, a bit sexy. My husband was at work now, so she was alone at home. I wondered why she was at home. Why was she not at work? How did she manage to survive? He was probably giving her money.

Yeah, I had to scrimp and save, working as hard as the Slave Isaura on the plantation from the Brazilian *telenovela* while she was sitting pretty at home and even more, was enjoying my man. Honestly, where was justice in this world?

And they didn't pay much at that laboratory. His wages for May were just paid, and it was August already. So, did it mean he was buying her flowers on my money?

Well, honey, I'll buy you flowers! From myself, personally, for your grave. Oh! Stop. That's not right. But on the other hand why not? She could get flowers, and I could not?

So, after piling up the agony I left the house, bought a bunch of red carnations, the most hideous flowers ever. Why did I do it? I couldn't answer. For the grave, probably. Whose grave, I couldn't say.

I couldn't remember exactly how I got to the right address. I knocked at the door.

A thin, short, homely woman opened the door. Even her teeth looked like a mouse's. I could knock those teeth out with one precise strike! How could he! For this gray mouse?

A wave of malicious joy and confidence in my success washed over me. I put a foot between the door and the jamb and with an impudent smile put out my hand, filled with those hideous carnations.

"Well, hello, Marina," I said.

The mouse's silent question in her face started changing into blue fear. She tried to close the door, but my determination and my foot stopped her.

"How will we talk? Either all the neighbors would hear, or in your apartment?" I asked. "I warn you, I'm going to speak very loudly. You see, I have a loud voice. Very loud."

I again turned on my all energy. Marina, with eyes full of horror, slowly opened the door and allowed me to enter. I continued to smile, and that probably comforted her enough for an expression of superiority to appear in her eyes. Or it seemed to me. In any case she said, "Aleksei told me you're beautiful. So, you're so beautiful, standing in front of me, in *my* house, and your husband prefers *me* to you. He doesn't want to live with a prostitute, even a beautiful one."

She shouldn't have said that. My right hand, still holding the bouquet of flowers, suddenly jerked, and *bam!* I punched that mouse right on the nose.

Previously I had fought only in my childhood, with boys, defending my toys and my child's dignity. There was no one to protect me; I had to do it myself. My mother wasn't faithful to my father, who was twenty-five-years her senior. She cheated on him. But when she nabbed him with a rodent like this, she left me, a nine-month-old baby, with her mother—my grandmother. She went off to manage her own life, and somehow forgot about me. So, as you can see, I was on my own.

If I remembered correctly, the last time I had punched anyone was when I was five-years-old.

Now I was dealing one blow after another until a couple of teeth fell on the wooden floor. The sound of fallen teeth brought me to my senses.

"Oh, the flowers look damaged. Well, never mind, they'll be perfect for the grave."

Abruptly swinging right around I left the apartment. I went outside and threw those flowers down at my feet. I left, and they, broken, but still alive, were abandoned, lying on the pavement. I had the feeling that someone was looking at me and shaking their head with disapproval. I looked around, but saw no one.

For the first time after a few months since I started suspecting Aleksei's betrayal, I felt relieved, even happy.

So that's what it was, that made me so happy: a sense of vengeance! The feeling of revenge!

But I did not know that when you take revenge on someone, you had to dig two graves at the same time. One for yourself.

In the meantime, jubilating, I tried to justify what I had done. She did not have to call me a prostitute. Who gave her that right? All I wanted was just a talk.

I was trying to justify myself, although subconsciously I knew it would have ended like this anyway. I didn't have any doubts, not even the smallest little thought of regret for what I had done. I did not even think what my precious hubby would say when he found out about everything.

Chapter Four

Aleksei's reaction was beyond my comprehension. I was expecting a ruckus, packing his stuff ostentatiously, and slamming the door. I was even ready for him to fight back, strike me, for his offended beloved.

But he said, "I understand. You were trying to protect your love and your family."

I couldn't even get one word out, I was so shocked by this statement.

"Yes, of course, you've crossed the line. Knocking two teeth out was too much. Those, however, were prostheses, but done in a very expensive clinic. She is going to file a charge against you."

I found my voice. "Well, she can try, if she wants the whole city to find out what I've slugged out her prostheses for. Anyway, let everyone know that she has a prosthesis instead of healthy teeth." And then I started laughing. And then I began to cry.

My hysterical laughter, mixed with sorrow and tears added fuel to the fire. But I didn't know that then.

Aleksei continued, "Marina said I had to give you a good thrashing, otherwise she would not stay with me. We were going to get married and move to Israel."

"Go ahead, and don't let the door hit you in the ass. And this applies to both of the planned actions."

"You know I cannot. I'm afraid that if I beat you, I'll kill you. I'm so much stronger than you. Though it didn't give you pause, that you are stronger than Marina."

"Am I stronger?"

I got up from the couch I was sitting on and approached the mirror. A cute, slim young woman looked from the other side. I flexed my arms, showing off my muscles. My arms were pretty skinny. I turned and looked at my profile over my shoulder. Then I dropped my arms.

"*Hmm*. You're probably right. I am stronger."

"But we have a son, and that's the important thing right now. Count yourself fortunate. You have won back your happiness. I'll stay with you."

That was benevolence uncharacteristic of him. He finally recollected that he had a son. In addition, Aleksei looked grief-stricken. And I suddenly realized that I didn't want him to stay with me. I wanted him to leave. Forever.

How could I get into bed with him, each time imagining that he had hugged and kissed this mouse? How would I continue to cook for him? How would I talk, look him in his eyes? How could I smile and pretend that nothing had happened? Instead, all I wanted was to feed him arsenic or cyanide.

Subconsciously, I felt that something was wrong. There was something so not typical of my husband in this exchange. But for the sake of my son, I tried to ignore any warning signals, to avoid breaking through to the resentment, my desecrated pride, and my broken heart.

———

There was no need, no desire to lie in the same bed with him. Whether he understood that I couldn't, or did not want to, he didn't make any attempt to get closer either. For me, life became almost unbearable, though now he came home on time. We politely talked to each other, but the atmosphere was extremely tense.

I felt a strange, almost tangible sense of an aculeate mass inside of me, as though an entire hive of wasps were in my chest that manifested whenever Aleksei came home. I felt that something would happen. Something was going to happen. Something terrible. What could I do to prevent this terrible something from happening? How? These were the questions that tormented my life now.

I had no one to ask.

Chapter Five

If you feel it's wrong to do something, it's better not to do it. Now, I know that because of our mentality to have everything in order, to be responsible and to organize our days, we have lost a very important quality: to listen to ourselves. For example, when we do not feel like eating, something in the body tells the brain, "I'm not hungry," but we still sit down and swallow a bowl of borscht, a cutlet with potatoes, and something after for dessert, because it's time for lunch. It's just a must to eat when it's lunchtime.

I was not an exception. I didn't know how to listen to myself. So when something in the morning was telling me, "Do not do anything today. Just spend the whole day in bed doing nothing," I didn't listen.

Yesterday I promised Aleksei I would burn the garbage, and then he could take what was left to the waste dump. The Perestroika, the period of "restructuring" was in full spate, and such things as municipal services were not important in the big picture. So there was no trash service. Even those who were duty-bound to take care of such services did nothing. And how could they, when such global issues as "rebuilding" were being resolved, people were to think about the common goal of better tomorrows and deal with trash by themselves in their backyards.

So people got fancy, getting rid of these wastes of civilization by using their imagination. I generally put the garbage in bags, and then burned those together with dry leaves. This time I planned to do the same.

Life seemed to have finally become somewhat normal. Sure, with Aleksei we lived as in the American joke, "My wife and I sleep in different beds. I sleep in New York, she sleeps in Michigan." We slept in different rooms. He went to work, came back home on time. We didn't talk of what had happened. We avoided eye contact. Perhaps we shouldn't have. Maybe, if I had looked deeply in his eyes, I would have seen something so terrifying that it would make me run as far away as possible.

Regardless all the forebodings, I got down to managing the trash. Vova was at home on school holidays, so he was helping me.

There was one more detail worth mentioning. A local priest from the village church was invited for lunch today. I met him in the courtyard of my neighbor, and wanted to ask for advice and God's blessings. But somehow, instead of cooking a nice meal for my guest, I was working in the backyard, because I'd told Aleksei I would.

This priest was the organizer of the demolition of Lenin's monument which, as expected, used to bristle in the center of the village in front of the village council. Everyone knew that Lenin was against religion and the church. He wrote many articles and books on the struggle against the opium of the people. By his order, a considerable number of churches, many of which were works of art, were destroyed. Father Illarion followed in the footsteps of the Leader of the Proletariat, and was trying to destroy the very idea of Lenin and Lenin himself, embodied in the granite sculpture. So he was kind of a warrior for the bright future, keeping pace with the times, fighting for the implementation of the ideas of Perestroika.

At those times the whole country eagerly took up the rebuilding idea: demolition of monuments, changing of street names, even names of entire cities. Big sums of money were spent on this, money that was taken from the salaries of teachers, doctors, and other workers.

One morning the village Chervona Sloboda woke up and all the Communist monuments were gone. Every single one. It soon became clear whose work that was and Father Illarion was arrested as a political offender. He stayed in the bullpen for three days, and was very proud to add this to his political past. People reached out to him and consequently the prestige and well being of the

Chervona Sloboda church quickly went up in the world and, consequently, Father Illarion's career.

———

It was August, two in the afternoon, and incredibly hot. Vova and I were both lightly dressed: shorts and T-shirts. I was happy because my son had voluntarily expressed a desire to help me, and I enthusiastically started my chore.

Since all the problems with his father started, my son had taken his side. When you are fifteen you don't really understand what's really going on. In addition, at this age boys are always closer to their fathers. I was so worried, I kept crying, arguing, and that was making everything even worse. Now I was quite happy that I had at least some sympathy and help from my son this afternoon.

Emptying the contents of the bag on the ground, I set it on fire. In the bag there was a lot of paper, newspapers, pieces of old wallpaper. The rubbish flamed up quickly, and the heap was getting smaller right before my eyes. My son went for a second trash bag, and I took a rake and began pushing all the burning pieces back into the heap. There were a couple of bottles and cans. One bottle was filled with some liquid and closed by a cork. The label read, OLIVE OIL. Strange! Could I really have thrown a full bottle of oil in the garbage? I should take it out of the fire, or else, God forbid, it could explode.

I walked over to get it out, and *ba-bam*!

I wasn't sure I had any thoughts of after that. All I knew was I just saw a huge ball of fire, and the fact that my legs were on fire. I tried to put it out with my hands, but it didn't help. There was a weird chemical smell and it was incredibly hard to breathe. For some reason, I suddenly had a sore throat.

Other than my throat, I didn't feel any pain, surprisingly nothing at all. A thought came into my head: If it doesn't hurt, maybe it's just a dream.

So there I was, quietly ready to accept that I was doomed to be burned alive. As though this were a funky dream I saw my son running towards me. He was saying something, but I could not understand a single word. He grabbed me by the arm and dragged me into the house. We reached it quickly and then it came. Pain.

It was unbearable, unrelenting! My son called the ambulance and then tried to help me, putting wet cloths on my feet, which had pieces of burnt skin all over them. I was moaning, too ashamed to cry. The ambulance took twenty minutes to arrive, when I was close to passing out. Unfortunately, I did not lose consciousness. I walked to the ambulance by myself. Then there was another torturous walk from the ambulance to the hospital staffroom, which was up the stairs on the second floor, and only there I was given a painkiller.

The doctors for some reason thought that someone had tortured me, and I was trying to explain how everything had happened, but because of the terrible pain and drugs my consciousness refused to obey me. The last thing I thought before switching off was, Thank God, at that moment my son had left for some more trash, and wasn't near me! Thanks be to God!

Chapter Six

That evening Aleksei did not show up at the hospital. I came to my senses a couple of times, and then again fell into a heavy, drugged sleep. They put me on an intravenous drip to wash the poison from the burnt tissue out of my body, but my heart stopped because of that.

My temperature shot up to 105.8. They were worried about my brain. I had to be given drugs intravenously to lower the fever, but that was also dangerous for my heart. I heard the doctors argue about something at my bedside, but I could not concentrate enough to understand what they were saying. In the end, on the edge of consciousness I caught that the doctors were split over my condition: some of them wanted to transfer me to a special burn ward in the regional hospital, while others were against such a transfer. The question was if I could survive such a transfer. For better or for worse, I stayed where I was.

Occasionally, coming to my senses, I saw Dr. Viacheslav Dmitrievich sitting at my bed, holding my hand and checking my pulse. Each time I tried to smile, but fell asleep again. As I learned later, he spent four days and nights like that, sitting in that chair.

I found out later I died at least a dozen of times during these four days. I depended for my life on this doctor, who sat by my bed all the time. Each time my heart failed to beat I was revived and brought back to life.

Finally, on the fifth day, I woke up blurred, my mind darkened, but sane. The doctors were doing the rounds. Approaching my bed they smiled, knowing that my young, though weak, body had defeated death.

"Good morning, butterfly! Wings still hurt?"

I burst into tears, not able to express any words of gratitude, knowing that no words could show how thankful I was. But the doctors, there were four of them, understood everything without words. They were happy because they were able to pull me out of the jaws of death.

"Today we have a double celebration," said Nikolai Ivanovich, the head of the department. "First of all, all together we've helped a pretty girl, Polina, come into the world of the living for the second time. And secondly, Viacheslav Dmitrievich is going on vacation. So, girl, behave yourself. Okay?"

He laughed and walked away. I felt as if I were lying under a train. It seemed like I weighed three hundred pounds. Not only my feet and legs hurt, but every cell of the body ached. My memory was returning, and I involuntarily began to recollect what had happened during these past four days. I couldn't remember seeing the man, with whom I spent seventeen years of my life, here by my bedside. But I had to quit trying to understand, and had to come back to reality.

I was recuperating from severe burns, beginning to heal, and that meant hunger. My body was starving for food, demanding the immense number of kilocalories required to repair massive thermal damage.

Chapter Seven

First, I made friends with the neighbors in my hospital ward. There were four of us. Sveta had both her legs in plaster, the result of a car accident, as I found out later. The driver turned out to be a decent man, and brought her to the hospital. He was paying for the necessary medicines, and even came to visit her.

Galia had been given a thrashing by her drunken husband. Doctors suspected concussion, so decided not to take any chances with that, and to keep her in the hospital as long as possible. Moreover, it was a nice opportunity for her husband to feel what it was like to live without borsch and a woman's love and care. He must have realized, one hundred percent, how hard it was, because he came to visit her five times a day, often bringing an apple or candy, and each time he swore until he was blind that this was the very last time he would drink vodka. Naive. But kind to Galia in her convalescence.

My third neighbor was Maria Vasilievna. Sveta called her Grandma Maria; Galia, Aunt Maria. I could not use any of the nicknames. They were so simple, while she looked so smart and intelligent. She was about eighty, and was here with a broken arm. Most of all I was struck by her eyes. She looked deep into your soul so attentively, I would say, tenaciously but kindly at the same time.

She looked at me with sympathy and interest. Well, everyone looked at me with interest, some with compassion. After all, I had made the whole village talk about me. I was a kind of local celebrity to them now.

I was still going over and over the past days, especially the first four, and was surprised that my memory did not catch a single instance of Aleksei's presence. What about Vova? Did Aleksei really not come to see me? Not even once? No, this couldn't be true. Probably I was asleep, I was on pain pills; of course I didn't remember! We had lived together for almost seventeen years, he wouldn't abandon me like this, defenseless, incapacitated, with burned legs. But as the proverb says, "Speak of the devil."

And I saw him. He was slowly and stealthily entering the ward. I still had fever, was in pain, and hunger of healing took away a lot of energy. He sat down at the foot of the bed, avoiding looking at me.

"How are you?"

"Not good yet. But the doctors said I would live." I even tried to smile.

"Don't tell me you how bad you feel, because I'm feeling worse than you!"

I couldn't understand a single thing he was saying. My ears weren't working. He was mumbling, his face turned away from me.

"After all, living with a cripple..."

"Why would you think that I would be a cripple?"

"Well, think about it. Your legs. And your face! Have you seen yourself in the mirror?"

I hadn't thought about my face. But at that moment I didn't want to look in the mirror.

"Leave," was the only thing I managed to say, hiding the tears rolling down my cheeks. Here it was—my payback.

And he left. As it turned out, forever. Or almost forever, but it would have been better if that had been the last time I saw him. The door closed behind my ex-husband, and I, holding back my tears, exhausted with fatigue, fell into broken slumber.

Chapter Eight

The atmosphere in the district hospital was quite friendly. The chief physician, with the not very euphonious last name – Krot, which means *mole* in Russian, was a great professional, and it seemed to me, a truly wise man. Throughout the region the hospital was well known for good outcomes and an excellent reputation. Not only the local high and mighty preferred to be treated here, important people came from all over Ukraine to this hospital.

Krot managed to hire a great team of doctors, nurses, and aides, and even managed to create decent working conditions for them. He paid them salaries, which was not a very common thing in those days. Even American humanitarian supplies, given to almost all medical institutions at that time, were actually kept and used in the hospital, not sold to put money into his own pocket.

But as congenial as he was, he could hold his subordinates accountable. Once I heard him giving advice to his doctors during one of the rounds, "Do your best to save your patients from suffering, they are already suffering enough just by being here." In my opinion, this wasn't something you would often hear from a doctor, though maybe I just had not come across such doctors.

———

No matter how you sliced it, on the way to my recovery I would face many obstacles that I would have to overcome and lessons I would have to learn by heart.

Next morning, after their rounds, our consulting physician, a man with incredible blue eyes and resembling Aramis in looks from *The Three Musketeers*, brought me a bottle of yellowish liquid, and another one with Novocaine. He gave me a shot of morphine, reminding me that today was the last day for this kind of easy pain relief, and that tomorrow I would have to live without it. After this he told me to free my legs from the bandages.

I sat up straight and looked at my legs. Lymph had seeped through the fabric, making my legs look like the bark of an old tree, all the way to my groin. Dr. Vladimir Ivanovich, my Aramis, said that those bandages were soaked with Novocaine to help relieve the pain from the burns. In addition, it was August outside, with swarms of flies everywhere. The doctors were afraid that one of these insects would start to fiddle while Rome was burning, landing on my wounds and carrying infection. So it was even more important to keep my wounds clean and covered. Dr. Aramis said he would check back on me in a few hours.

Generously pouring from both bottles, the Furacilin and the Novocaine, on my feet, unable to hold my tears within, I started to free my lower extremities from the sodden fabric. This torture lasted no less than two-and-a-half hours, and the result horrified me.

There was no skin on my feet! There was no skin on my legs! In a few places, I saw pieces of white "cloth," which turned out to be bits of my skin. The burnt areas were shimmering with red, black, and pink colors, and in some places I could even see a white bone.

The tears were suffocating me as I uncovered at my legs. Once these legs had attracted the opposite sex at all levels and all sectors of the population. According to the roughest statistical calculations, this part of my body always got the most compliments, starting with the most sophisticated phrases, and ending with "I'm going to get lost in those legs tonight," generally adding the crudest of gestures and facial expressions.

My companions in misfortune didn't stop me from crying. They offered no sympathetic phrases. They knew that not everyone could handle such a reality without tears. But Aramis, when he found me in tears, was surprised.

"Does it hurt?"

"No," I said.

"Then why are you crying?"

I could not explain, but continued sobbing. The doctor, clearly not understanding my tears, got right down to redressing my legs. He, unlike me, seemed to be quite satisfied with what he saw. "Good," he kept saying. "Great!" What exactly was good and great, I did not see. Exhausted after such work, the horror of disfigurement, and under the sway of the morphine, I fell asleep.

I woke up a few hours later with a strong feeling that I'd learned my first lesson.

I realized that this nightmare was happening for a reason. There was only one person to blame. Myself.

Chapter Nine

I didn't know where such thoughts came from, but I did not try to understand. I knew for certain this was my punishment for all the dark and wrong I had done in my life, and I had to go through it. And I knew that the way I would overcome this would influence my future life. Or death.

I decided to become stronger. How? I had no idea. But I was absolutely convinced that I had only two choices: to become strong or to die. I did not want to die. I began to recollect all the people who, according to my limited academic knowledge, were considered strong. Zoya Kosmodemyanskaya, a Soviet partisan and a Hero of the Soviet Union. She had to die before she got her award. So I didn't want to be exactly like her. There was Alexey Maresyev, a Soviet fighter ace during World War II, and even Jeanne D'Arc. Well, but poor Joan was burned at the stake. I had already tried that.

I soon discovered that I still had my guardian angel, my nurse Vera. It was she, a woman from a small village, impressed by my usual self-control, who changed my bandages two and three times a day, changed my sheets, covered with medicine and pus from burnt flesh, and kept repeating, "My little warrior, a little more patience. Impressive: not a single tear, not a word, or a groan. You are a warrior, like Zoya Kosmodemyanskaya."

I didn't consider myself a warrior, but when I came to know Nurse Vera better, I was surprised and astonished by her strength, endurance, and wisdom.

In a conversation with this wonderful and compassionate woman, I found out that she was a witness to my arrival at the hospital. She saw as I walked by myself from the ambulance to the emergency room, and then, on the second floor, those little white flags of skin dotting my legs. She was astonished that I was moving under my own steam, trying to get up the stairs, without making a single sound.

It was she, the mother of two sons, both of whom were in the war in Afghanistan, who, neither by word nor look, showed her fear for the lives of her children. It was Vera who helped me survive and get back on my feet. She taught me to walk again. In the two months that I couldn't get up from the hospital bed, she was my nurse, my friend, and my support.

Thank you, Vera! I know your children will return to you safe and sound, and one day you will dandle your grandchildren on your knee, because you deserve them.

Only three people were in my life during this period. There was Vera. There was my son, who at fifteen managed to support a household consisting of three purebred dogs, chickens, rabbits, and a vegetable garden. He even tried to spoil his mom once in a while with something tasty he had cooked.

There was a third person I had not expected any help from. And therein was the second lesson I had to learn and comprehend. What kind of people did I surround myself with in my life? Whom did I trust? What did I learn from them? Where the heck were those people I could rely on? Were there any at all? Who were those people who were worthy to be called friends?

There were not that many. But they helped me as much as they could. Some friends brought me watermelons, to wash out poisons that had seeped into my blood from the burned tissues. Thanks to Heaven it was August!

Another friend sent almost a whole bucket of Vishnevsky liniment balm for wound healing. Alexander Vishnevsky was a doctor, long before there were antibiotics. It was due to him and his smelly birch sap and fish oil ointment that I avoided surgery and skin transplantation, to the big surprise of all the hospital doctors. God bless this Vishnevsky! I'm sure he was a strong and intelligent man.

So many people I knew, who I had truly believed to be my friends, didn't appear at all. Or they came once out of curiosity, to make sure that this was not a rumor and that I really got so badly burnt that I couldn't get out of bed. Some started sniveling immediately after opening the door of my ward, shedding crocodile tears. Why crocodile? Why because I nipped in the bud such expression of feelings. And their "tears" immediately dried up.

"Stop, stop. It's already bad enough without your wailing. I'm the one in pain, not you."

I think they gratefully accepted what I asked of them, that they did not have to pretend to care about me. And there was no doubt they were pretending. First of all, I just felt it, and secondly, after a short visit and passionate promises to come back and bring something to read, or to help me, for example, by washing my hair, they disappeared. It was about such people that I had read in one of Veller's books: "A few more friends like this and I will not need enemies." One could never rely on such people.

I also remembered what Dr. Zviagin taught his desperate heroes in Veller's novels: To desire. To believe. To act.

As for me I was trying to learn by my own experience that I could rely only on myself. And very few friends. And believe me that was no less painful than the burnt skin. My soul was in pain, my mind was suffering.

How did it happen that I had surrounded myself with people indifferent and selfish? I must have been like that myself.

And now I had to figure out what needed to be changed in me. And how to surround myself with people from whom I could learn from to be truly sincere and wise. Wise as the old lady in my ward, Maria Vasilievna.

Surprising myself, I didn't take umbrage at people I communicated with at this time. Just the opposite. I clearly understood that the person had the right to live and act as he or she wanted. To be what he or she wanted, and not what I wanted them to be. Let everyone be what they want to be, that's what I decided. And only if they think that is not good enough and decide to change themselves or their attitude, they should do it. No one should force them. They should do it only as their own choice.

I realized that it was necessary to think about what I needed to be like for the people around me to feel comfortable and happy.

It all was my fault. I didn't manage to keep those who were wiser and smarter than me nearby; I hurt them, and now was paying for that. But I would try very hard. I'd find them and ask for forgiveness. And if they forgave me, I would try to make sure that they never had a reason to take offense with me ever again.

So that's how, after torturing myself with many thoughts and much heartache, instead of all these unreliable and indifferent people, I got one person in my life whose title was Best Friend.

Chapter Ten

Natasha began to visit me every day as soon as she learned what a misfortune had happened to me. She was a nurse, and either because of her professional habits or her moral virtues, she travelled from the other side of the city after her round-the-clock shift in the cancer hospital to visit. She didn't snivel, never lathered false sympathy onto me. But she did her best to entertain me with meaningless stories, news, and jokes. She washed my hair and wiped my face and hands with a cloth soaked in warm soapy water. But most importantly Natasha came every day and kept talking, talking, and talking. Telling me the news, keeping me in touch with the outside world.

I saw how tired she was, and asked not to come every single day, but she came anyway. In addition, she was checking on Vova and helped him with the household.

I had known her for a long time. She lived nearby and we used to walk our dogs on the same World War II tank training area that was now a park. She had an Afghan hound, and I had my three—a German shepherd and a pair of Russian borzois, all top of their class in national dog shows. We were pals, but without ever getting too deep into each other's lives.

Natasha called me one day and suggested we take our dogs out to the field, "to catch bunnies," as we called it. Our dogs were not able to catch anything like that, but a long run would be good for their health. As soon as we went and removed the leashes, they sped away and disappeared behind the hill. We were not really worried, we just kept talking, and following the same direction our dogs had taken. From the top of the hill we saw Vesta,

Natasha's Afghan, squirming on her back with enormous plea-sure. My Onega was nearby, eating something horrible, with an incredible appetite.

"Oh!"

"Not again!" We cried out almost simultaneously.

"Again, some stinky carrion!" Natasha was stupefied.

"Eating poop again!" I exclaimed.

And we rushed to our pets. I must say that hunting hounds like ours retain some habits of their wild predator ancestors. With such actions, the dogs destroy the smell of the delicious shampoos that the loving owners use for washing them, so the sweet scent does not prevent them from a successful hunt.

We walked home with dignity and pride, but at the same time trying not to breathe in too deeply. Night was coming, so the benches in the yards near the entrances were already occupied by curious old ladies, retirees who loved to know all the local news, discussed the gossip, and were always anxious to give advice to the guilty ones who passed their bench. That was a rule of socialist reality: never be indifferent to the shortcomings of others.

But that night, everything was going its special way. As soon as the old ladies saw our silhouettes in the distance, they opened their mouths as usual, to scold us for wasting money on feeding such huge dogs, but not our own children. But as the "fragrance" from our four-legged creatures reached them, their mouths were shut instantly. Immediately after, the old women disappeared into their apartments to hide from the unbearable stench. We had no other choice but to continue our journey home and pretend that nothing was happening.

Poor grannies! I could only imagine the many things they wanted to tell us, what they thought of Natasha and me.

Once we got home we washed our dogs with shampoo, with soap, and then again with shampoo, trying to get the stink out. I even tried to brush Onega's teeth. But the stench was so strong that we had to punish our pets, by closing them off on the balconies of our apartments. The nasty smell disappeared in a couple of days only after we repeated bathing them two or three times per day.

Now, recalling this incident on my hospital bed, we laughed our tails off.

Laughter, and the solicitude of now truly close and caring people put me back on my emotional feet. It also helped me to know who was not truly caring.

One day, about a month after the explosion, I noticed that, by biting the bullet, it was possible to hang my legs over the side of the bed. It made me so happy that I started doing that ten times a day. Meanwhile, life in the ward was taking its course. Everyone was busy with her own recuperation.

Maria Vasilievna continued, with curiosity, to watch my attempts to get back on my feet. And one day she said, "Polina, honey, do you want to tell me about that dream that you saw three days before the explosion?"

"But how do you know that, Maria Vasilievna? I didn't tell anyone about it. Was I delirious under the drugs?"

"No, you did not say anything." She smiled. "How do I know? Does it matter? So, do you want to tell me?"

That night just Maria and I were in the ward, and I decided to tell her about my dream. I thought there must be something special in her that made her look at me like that. She was clearly not your usual old lady. Moreover, she was going to be discharged tomorrow. So, why not tell her?

Perhaps I was ready for it, because each word that woman told me that night vibrated within me. I would remember them forever. And so, I told her my dream.

"I came back again to my city. It was a sunny summer's day. As usual, I came down the tail of the streets that formed the letter Y, a strange, incomplete crossroads. I had two hounds on the leash—Onega and a very beautiful black male dog. People were scurrying around. A lot of people. They were dressed in bright clothes and looked very busy. Some of them were selling things, others were buying them. Some were hurrying somewhere, others were having conversations.

"I decided that I finally wanted to learn about this city, the name of this street, and who lived in the gray stone building. I tried to talk to several people, but it seemed as though they didn't pay any attention to me or my dogs.

"I thought I needed to take a closer look around and search for some of my friends. And suddenly everyone began to scatter in different directions, running to their houses and closing the doors and shutters. Perplexed, I watched this stampede, trying to ask what was happening, but everyone looked at me with horror in their eyes, as though I had caused this panic.

"In a few minutes I was left totally alone with my dogs, at the intersection of the roads. It became completely silent, and then I felt a distinct tremor in the earth, as if an incredibly huge dinosaur was walking on the pavement, coming toward me. My dogs tensed, going on full alert. Step by slow earthshaking step, the thing came toward us.

"From around the corner there appeared an extraordinarily large and beautiful black bull with silver horns. It halted thirty feet from me. I was surprised, but for some unexplainable reason, not scared. I admired it. It was so beautiful, so powerful. Its eyes were bloodshot, its black body glistened in the sun, and its silver horns looked perfect. It was both terrifying and wonderful, and I could not take my eyes off of it. The black bull also seemed to stare at me and then slowly began to approach.

"Everything else in my dream was wrapped in an intense silence. I could hear only the sound of his hooves. And then I began to worry. Frightened, I began to look for some place to hide, instantly realizing it was useless to try. Then suddenly my black dog, tearing the leash out of my hand, raced toward the bull.

"'No,'" I cried. "Come here, right now! I slapped my hip, but he ignored his training.

"The dog ran up to the bull, and, as if teasing it, ran around to the left. The angry creature chased him. Onega ran after them, and I realized I was left alone.

"I had to get them away from that creature and make sure they were safe.

"For some reason I didn't think of myself. I ran after them, shouting, and looking for help. Onega came back to me after a while, but my Black Defender did not. I wandered around the city until nightfall. I called and called for him, weeping from my feelings of unbearable guilt. I was so sorry, and I knew that something terrible had happened to my dog.

"When I awoke, my face was wet with tears. My heart was heavy inside of me. I could hardly breathe because my throat was closing up with grief. I had lost someone dear and beloved. That feeling has never left me."

"I thought so," replied Maria Vasilievna, after a rather long pause. "I have something to say to you, but please, do not ask me anything. I will tell you only what I can tell. The rest you will understand yourself. If not now, then later. So, listen."

She leaned toward me.

"I've been watching you all this time, and I know you are not a simple person, and there is a reason why your life is filled with so many difficulties. Everything happens for a reason, but if you do not change yourself, your attitude towards people and life, you will die. The black bull is your death. You were supposed to die.

"And the black dog that saved you was your guardian angel. You lost him that night. He had vowed to watch over you, even to the cost of his life, to give you another chance. But now you have to live without him.

"I do not know exactly what is wrong in your life, if it's something you've done that was wrong, or done incorrectly. Or perhaps something you haven't done."

I burst into tears. They suddenly start rolling out of my eyes like a hall from the sky. I covered my face with palms. Shoulders began to shudder. First gently, then more and more. Eventually I started to cry like a little girl of five years old.

"I don't know what I've done to deserve this. I don't know," I whispered, not certain I was making any sound. But Maria Vasilievna heard me, because, with a sad smile, she continued. "And have you done any good? You know, in this life it's not enough not do anything wrong. Apparently, you have a mission that you must fulfill. In fact, you're a kind and clever girl, no doubt. But now you'll have to prove that you understand every-thing and are ready to change. It will be very difficult, very hard, because you no longer have your defender. You didn't notice him, didn't listen to him, you betrayed him, but he still believed in you and sacrificed his life for the sake of your salvation.

"But if you can, if you manage to get through all the difficul-ties and change yourself, he, your guardian angel, will revive like a phoenix and come back to you. But you have to prove your worth with all of your actions, and even your thoughts, that you deserve this."

I would not have predicted anything this woman had said. I was expecting some of the usual platitudes, stories about God, church, life. But such depth and awareness in her conversation! I was greatly surprised.

"I'm sorry, Maria Vasilievna, but to whom should I prove myself?"

"Darling, I said no questions. But I'll answer this one. I think that you have to prove it to yourself. As soon as you learn how to honestly and sincerely look yourself in the eyes, or rather, in your heart, you'll know it. You will understand everything. And your life will change. Very much. If you do not manage to do this, then, as I said, you will die. And let that not frighten you, either. Everyone dies. This is normal. Natural."

Maria Vasilievna smiled, a little sad, but somehow at the same time, so filled with light.

———

I did not know why, but I believed every word from this strange woman, even though all my life I was persuaded that the world was material. There were no angels, especially not guardian angels. Everything told to me today by this woman was strange, even ludicrous to me, but I believed it. [I saw that she was talking about things I had been wondering about for many years.]Somehow, I believed every word and I knew that if I did not listen to her now, I would die. So I did pay attention, very carefully. I wanted to live.

Besides, I suddenly recollected a man I had met in college. But just then I wasn't so certain that he was a man.

Chapter Eleven

At the time I was studying at Uman Teacher Training School, hoping to devote my life to the communistic education of the younger generation. I was a good student, but as always, I wanted to be loved and needed, which, again, as always, created problems for me.

One day I was walking along the central square of the glorious city of Uman with one of the most popular girls. Liuda, my good friend, was very beautiful according to the standards of those times, and my own idea of a beautiful woman. Large, expressive eyes, perfect eyebrows, a high, clean forehead, and long silken hair. I wasn't jealous of her looks, but I also wanted to be the same—beautiful, popular, and desired. I did my best. Now, I do not recall where we were going, but I definitely remember this feeling of admiration and pride I always felt near her. Such a beautiful girl as my friend!

A man was walking from the opposite direction. He looked terrible. So pale. Very pale. His skin was covered with spots and scabs. At least that's how I saw him. The man was almost bald, and the little bit of gray, and white hair only emphasized the pale color of his face. He looked as if he just came out from the grave. It gave me the creeps when he started talking. His voice was hollow and weak and sounded as if he'd just crawled out from a crypt.

"You," he said, turning to my girlfriend, "will have a difficult, not very happy life. Your daughter is going to be your Damocles' sword, but it will be your own fault."

"And you," he looked at me with his pale blue, almost colorless eyes, "you will be rich, loved, and happy."

I thought he even smiled a little. And then he just walked away. Liuda said nothing.

"This can't be happening!" I was stunned, and turned around to take another look at him and ask him who he was, but the man had disappeared.

"Did you see how scary that man was?" I asked Liuda.

"What man?"

"The one that has just passed by."

"Are you okay, Polina? I didn't see anyone!"

How could it be, I thought then, that she didn't see him? Probably she just didn't pay attention. Anyway, who was beautiful Liuda and who was I? How could it happen that she would be unhappy, and me, rich and loved.

Later, when life was particularly hard, after I understood much of what had to be understood, I thought about this strange man. With bitterness. Back then I really wanted to believe it was not a hallucination: that prophets did exist, and that happiness, wealth, and love were waiting for me. But what was happening to me was anything but happiness, wealth, or love. It couldn't have been just a delusion, I thought sometimes. Or could it?

Now, after this unexpected conversation with Maria Vasilievna, I remembered, for some reason, that strange man. And I believed both him and her.

"Maria Vasilievna, please, just one question. Only one."

"Depends on the question," the woman said.

"Tell me, this explosion, was it an accident, or was someone trying to kill me?"

"No, it was not an accident. There are no accidents. But the person who tried to do it was only an instrument, and you have to forgive him."

"Who is it?"

"Well, my dear, I will definitely not tell you that."

"Do you know who that was?"

"Yes, of course. But I cannot tell you. And I don't want to. I do not want to plant any seed of hatred and vengeance in your soul. Though, you will know who it is, and it will be better for you if you forgive that person."

"Forgive him? But will he, this almost-killer, bear any punishment?"

"Oh, he will. But, believe me, you will not want him to undergo that punishment."

"What? Why wouldn't I want him to pay for his crime? He tried to kill me!"

"You'll see, my dear. Sometimes life is so confusing and difficult. But remember, your future depends on the rectitude of your decisions. And not only *your* future, as you will see someday for yourself."

Those words were spoken with finality. Maria rummaged around in the basket of fruit that her friend had brought. And she handed me a perfectly ripe apple.

"Here, take this. Very tasty apples this time."

And she spoke no more of my dream.

Chapter Twelve

The next day, Maria Vasilievna was discharged and another woman became my ward neighbor. Her name was Olga Soroka. She was very sick, in a severe stage of diabetes, and terrible gangrene was spreading all over her legs. So it was only Svetlana, with her legs plastered, and me now.

Svetlana couldn't get up from bed by herself. I was doing my first unsure steps with the help of Vera, my hospital angel. I felt so dizzy during each of these attempts that I could not keep my balance. Something must have happened to my brain; I had no idea what part of my body I needed to move to take a step.

That's probably how God created the world. First, there was an idea. The same for me, first a thought: what to do, what muscles to use to put my right foot in front of my left. Okay, good, I would say, talking myself through it. Then I needed somehow to transfer my body weight onto the right leg, and on it would go from there. Step by step, with the help of my teachers, I learned to walk again. Was it as hard to learn how to walk when I was a child? I didn't remember.

This is really when you start appreciating the simple actions that are available to you. You learn to enjoy the little things that are given to you together with your life. "Be grateful and rejoice in all that surrounds you," says one of the cosmic laws. I was grateful. Very grateful. And it was another lesson I had learnt.

Learning to walk was progressing quite well, and on the third day I could take a few independent steps. It was still very painful, but the joy of success and the pride from my achievements made me overcome this pain. So, the first challenge completed, I thought to myself. I was happy and thanked those who had helped, the doctors, and everyone around me.

When I met Olga Soroka, life with my pain seemed a picnic compared to the suffering of that poor woman. That was the next lesson to learn: Everything in this world is relative.

Olga was being prepared for double leg amputation, but the diabetes made doctors keep postponing it. They were expecting Olga's daughter to come by to discuss the potential consequences of the operation. Perhaps even her mother's death.

But her daughter was not in a hurry to come for a visit, even though Olga was brought to the hospital emergency room by ambulance on a Saturday night.

Additionally, in the emergency, Maria forgot to bring her medicines, and as ill luck would have it, at that moment there was nothing in the hospital that could stand in as replacements.

Her first night in the ward, this poor woman could not sleep a wink. It was hot. The flies were swarming to the terrible odor coming from her legs, especially strong when she changed the bandages. She cried and moaned all night. On Sunday morning the admitting physician tried to do everything he could, first, to keep her alive until Monday, and second, to somehow to ease her suffering. Svetlana and I also did our best to support the poor woman, demonstrating our recovery and firmly promising Olga that by next week we would all be up and dancing, if not to rock and roll then at least some 7:40 with the klezmer or some Sirtaki from *Zorba the Greek*.

Olga's daughter didn't come Sunday, either. In the evening, exhausted from pain and suffering, Olga begged me to call her daughter, and to see if she would bring her medication to the hospital. She wrote a phone number on a piece of paper, and thus I went into the first crusade of my new life, down the hallway, some thirty or forty feet. To me it seemed like a mile over broken glass. Carefully, supporting myself with the wall, I reached the nurse's station where the phone sat on the desk.

Olga's daughter picked up the phone and replied that she would not be able to come today, because her husband was celebrating something with the neighbors, so he couldn't drive. And she herself was too tired after work and therefore would arrive only the next day, so she asked me to just to say hello to her mother for her. When I told Olga that, she burst out weeping, and said medicine would be of much better use than her daughter's one word greeting.

At eleven p.m. that night, Olga Soroka died. Before our very eyes.

"Her heart gave out" Dr. Savchenco said, " Poor women. Even her own daughter abundant her. Die alone. How awful".

"How awful! That's it! Olga wasn't that bad as I was". Thoughts in my head swarmed like bees. They buzzed and worn in different directions, bumping into one another. " Her daughter just didn't realize that her mom was that bad. I'm pretty sure. But my husband! I was almost dead if Dr. Vyacheslav Dmitrievich didn't go home for several days. How could he abundant me, leave me to die? Or he hoped that I will die? Right. Then he don't need to get divorce and share the stuff we collected living together. No arguing. No fighting. No Problem. He probably likes the word "no". Well, no. I am alive. I will get well and will live happily ever after.

This was the first time I'd ever seen anyone die. It was one of the biggest horrors—to see a person dying right in front of you and not being able to help!

Next two hours Svetlana and I spent in the ward with the deceased Olga. Such were hospital rules: a dead person had to be left for two hours in the ward. Perhaps to be sure they were well and truly passed on. At one a.m. the doctors finally wheeled Olga out and wished us good night.

How could we have a good night after watching Olga die, neglected by her own daughter? We were both in shock. We couldn't even talk at first. I knew that was another lesson. And I had to learn it by heart: Hurry to live, otherwise it may be too late. Tomorrow may not come.

Hurry up to live; otherwise it may be too late! Go visit the person you want to see. Say a kind word to him or her or you may run out of time to say it. You'll regret it all your life, blame yourself, but it will be impossible to change anything! Anything at all.

———

After a while our senses started coming back. Moreover, the doctor on duty that night was the young, but already highly experienced physician and nice person, Alexander Savchenko.

"Why aren't you sleeping, girls?"

"Well, it's too hard to accept the recent events."

"Yes, I understand. So sorry it happened this way. Anyway, I will not turn off your lights for now. Even better, I have something that will distract your attention. I know it's been a tough experience."

And he brought us a half-full bottle of a wonderful wine called Cahors.

In a village, everything is always much simpler, I would even say more sincere than in the city. People do not pay attention to the unimportant things, such as the gift being only half a bottle. They just accept with gratitude the fact that people want to help.

Not every Ukrainian medical institution has doctors who offer wine to their patients! But in this small hospital there was a home-like atmosphere with a lot of kindness and empathy. Along with professionalism and strict rules for following medical procedure, you would meet cordiality and generosity of spirit. Of course, the chief physician might not be completely happy to hear about anything like this, but I'm sure he would understand.

Dr. Savchenko had even brought clean water glasses.

"Here, girls, let's have a glass for the peace of Olga Soroka's soul. A remedy for your exhausted minds."

Svetlana and I couldn't believe it. But the wine was great, and toasting Maria helped us both to accept her passing. After that, the doctor poured us half of glass of wine each, and advised us to switch to some more optimistic topics. We relaxed a bit but still couldn't sleep, of course. And then suddenly, *thunk-thunk, thunk-thunk, thunk-thunk*!

Svetlana and I froze, in the full sense of the word.

I wasn't sure what Svetlana was thinking at that moment, but I suddenly said, "Svetlana, what if Soroka didn't die? She was taken to the morgue, where she came back to life, and now, *now* she is coming back for us!"

"Do you think she's angry with us?" Svetlana asked.

"What for?"

"Well, I don't know. Maybe because we're still alive?"

"She has no reason to be cross with us." I tried to look brave. "We did call her daughter. Right? It's not our fault she refused to come to her mother's side."

Fear enchained us. We could not move and just stared at the door. I didn't know what we expected to see there. The dead Maria Soroka coming, staggering on her gangrenous legs.

Then the sound of something creaking added fuel to the fire.

And then we both began to shake with silent hysterical laughter. The only fridge available on our floor was just in front of our ward. Apparently one of the patients wanted to have a drink of cold water or something, and had thumped down the hall. Another lesson to learn. Very often, along with sad, even tragic events, there is something comical or funny. For equilibrium and balance I guess.

———

Five-thirty a.m., and still we could not sleep.

At about seven in the morning, Svetlana and I finally fell asleep, and were woken up at nine by somebody screaming. No, it was not screaming. It was a cry of rage. When I opened my eyes, I saw it was a woman who was raging inside our ward. It took me a moment to realize that she was directing this anger at me.

"Why in the name of all that's holy didn't you tell me my mother was so bad that she might die!"

And then her language became much worse. At first I was taken aback, just half-awake after a few hours of sleep. I opened my mouth to return her anger, and then I realized what was going on. The doctors were standing next to her with their heads down. I felt, quite unexpectedly, absolutely calm.

I gave her the time to cry out all the grief. After all, her mother died. And then, very quietly, I said, "Well, as you see, I already got what I deserve. And you, my dear, will someday get yours."

Everyone looked at me, completely dumbfounded. And she, Maria's daughter, stood with her mouth open. Perhaps she also understood something in what I had said.

Everyone left. Everyone, except me and Svetlana. We *couldn't* leave.

Later the same day Svetlana went home for a week. Then they brought her back only to remove the plaster. Her young body coped perfectly, the bones healed beautifully. I never saw her after, but I hoped that everything was going smoothly in her life. She was young, beautiful, and seemed to be surrounded by caring people and God's blessings.

As for me I was just starting my path in a new life. Both literally and figuratively speaking, I was taking my first steps. At the age of forty.

Chapter Thirteen

The number forty, in my opinion, has some mysterious meaning. In the Bible, forty days and forty nights of rain removed life from earth. Moses was on Mount Sinai for forty days and forty nights. In fairy tales this number is mentioned a considerable number of times, as in the story "Ali Baba and the Forty Thieves."

Commemoration for the dead is performed on the fortieth day. A woman carries a child for forty weeks. And what about the phrase "forty times forty," which is so much of something that it can't be counted?

Did you think that that number, my age of forty, had no particular significance? Well, I disagree. My second life began at forty. And it was truly one rough, potholed road of a beginning. And it only got worse after I was finally discharged from the hospital and sent home.

From the first, I noticed that I could not turn on a gas stove and cook anything. There I was, hungry, standing in front of a stove, looking at it, but I couldn't light it.

Before I was burnt, I thought I knew what fear was, but I was wrong. Never before had I felt such a horror as standing in front of that stove, the horror growing inside of me until I fainted.

I began to black out each time I was frightened. And I was scared of everything: a phone call, loud voices, fire, but also terrified even of water. And every time: *boom!* I would collapse. I would lose consciousness five and six times a day, beaten black and blue by the floor at the end of each day. The doctors called this dystonia, as in vegetative-vascular dystonia and migraine, all a result of the thermal injuries.

Next, I found out that I had no job anymore. Redundant. Of course, I was paid some severance money, due to the staff reduction, but, first of all, the sum was so ridiculously small that one could burst her sides with laughing at it, and secondly, I was still jobless. There was nothing to help me feed my family. At least what was left of it.

However, I had no strength to do anything. And no husband to support me. Only my son was happy that I was still alive and back home, and Natasha continued to come and help me out.

The next surprise was that it was impossible to find a job. Turned out that in our country no one needed you if you were forty. All the interviews ended after the question, "How old are you?" It was difficult to actually understand why retirement was popularly considered to be the most productive time of a person's life, but those, like me who had never taken so much as maternity leave, had gained experience and life wisdom, suddenly became not needed. But, unfortunately, that's how everything was.

My son entered military college. He wanted to follow in the footsteps of his great-grandfather, Vasily, who did military service during World War II. He had been quite unlucky. After being a part of the army that had helped the Soviet Union to hang out its flag of victory in Berlin, he was sent to Japan to fight some more.

However, he returned home alive and more or less healthy, and able to live the rest of his life with honor and dignity. Vasily Pavlovich lived for eighty-three years, enjoying the world he had won at the cost of his own blood, spending time with his great-grandson Vovochka, whom he loved more than his children and grandchildren. And he even wrote his memoirs.

After my son left for college I was all alone. On the one hand, it was great to finally have a chance to take care of no one but myself. On the other hand, I felt so lonely, abandoned, and forgotten by everyone.

But even that was not enough. Aleksei demanded that I sell the house and pay him part of the money from the common property settlement. In addition, he tried to persuade our son to give him *his* share.

But he didn't want Vova to go live with him or even visit him at Marina's apartment. Aleksei just wanted to see his own son once in a while, when it was convenient.

It was almost impossible to sell the house, with so many people out of work. I had no income to pay for gas and electricity. An incredible amount of debt had accumulated since my ex-husband stopped getting paid. But Aleksei didn't care. He was not going to pay for anything.

"Well, I have no money! Where should I find it?" he shouted at me.

In short, these became everyday squabbles. Everyday agonies that proved how abandoned I was.

My neighbors on either side realized that I was alone and there was no one to protect me. Vulnerable. They kept trying to cut off a piece of land on each side. At night they moved the border on my vegetable garden inward each from their own borders, in order to claim three more feet of my yard. I fought for my land as a warrior, but the corrupt land surveyor was not in a hurry to stand up for justice and help me. The court system was also not the best in the world, so the neighbors stole part of my land, despite all the documentation available. Another misfortune in my life at that time, my age of forty. My life was hell.

Chapter Fourteen

But hell itself was not all those problems. I didn't live in hell; hell lived in me. *Hatred.* I hated so much when I thought about my past life or my ex-husband. Heaven forbid that someone should pronounce the name *Aleksei* in my vicinity. Each time I felt that tons of bricks were falling onto me. Yes, yes, red and heavy, with sharp angles—bricks. I physically felt the pain when they each "fell" on my head, my shoulders, and my back. I would not be surprised if there could be anything but bruises left on my skin. Automatically I cowered and covered my head and face with my hands. It was hard to breathe. Mostly it ended up with my losing consciousness. My hatred grew and flourished with each passing day. Who allowed him to destroy my life? All I've achieved in my life destroyed. So much hard work and so many sleepless nights! How many times I stinted myself to please the one I loved!

Soon I began to develop a plan of revenge in my head.

I could neither eat nor sleep, nor live. Hatred settled in my heart, my soul, occupied my entire mind. It seethed and multiplied. It was impossible to think of anything else but how to make Aleksei and Marina go through the hell I was in. But no, that would not be enough! It was necessary to make them suffer more, so that they eventually died.

The Marina-mouse lived on the ground floor. I could probably throw a grenade or a bomb in their window at night. Or use the same inflammable mixture which had almost killed me. I was even thinking of getting into their apartment at night, tying them up and then slowly torturing the two of them. Make them beg me for their lives.

My God, I prayed, I am not capable of such things.

But I could also hire a hit man, said my hatred.

I had no idea where I was going to get a grenade or a bomb, how I would I tie them up, not to mention actually perform tortures. Where would I even get money for the hit man? But I couldn't think of anything else. I knew, with certainty, I would never be able to do anything like that, but I kept thinking it and thinking it.

Young brides called, I did their beautiful hairstyles and applied stunning make-up, but because of this all-consuming hatred I couldn't remember any of the young faces. I stopped sleeping, lost my appetite. I became skinny, nervous, and angry.

There were still no buyers for the house. Aleksei regularly called and demanded his money for it. Each time he nagged me it fed my hatred. Furthermore, I missed my son terribly. And I felt sorry for him. I imagined it would feel so good to turn my ex over to the police, and make him pay for everything by sending him to jail. The house issues would be solved automatically. And my vengeance would be accomplished, but how would my son live with the knowledge that his father was in prison thanks to his mother? For trying to murder his mother. It would kill him and make him suffer from hatred toward those who gave him life.

Believe me, I knew what that was like. Neither my father nor my mother wanted me. I never saw my father. Then my mother left, and then somehow forgot all about me and wiped me out of her life. All my life I was trying to prove to the whole world that I was a good person. Why didn't they want me? Why didn't they like me? My complexes multiplied, as the shells on the bottom of an old boat, creating the well-known inferiority complex.

How could I even dare to think to take vengeance on the father of my son? I myself chose this man to be his father. Maria Vasilievna was absolutely right, "I am afraid you will not want him to be punished."

I tried prayer. Oh God, what should I do? How should I live with this? What is the way out?

So another year passed.

———

But one day, it was a wonderful summer's day. It was the middle of the week. The next Saturday there was supposed to be a wedding of a lovely girl, Zhenia. We agreed that today, this beautiful summer's day, at seven p.m., to meet at her house to look at the dress and accessories, and to discuss hairstyle and make-up for the ceremony.

Zhenia was living in one of the most unique residences in our city. The fourteen-story building, built by Yugoslavians using some new architectural techniques, was in the heart of the city. I was there on time, but Zhenia wasn't home yet.

I went up to the fourteenth floor balcony to look out over the city in all of its green summer glory, and suddenly realized, "Here it is—the solution! Jump and that's it. Finished! No more problems. No debts. No house to sell in order to give money to the man I hated. And there would be no need for revenge because my suicide would be the best revenge. Could anyone live after realizing that someone had killed herself because of you?

What a relief it would be. No more humiliation, no need to try to convince your potential employer that you were not too old for the job, but, on the contrary, more experienced and better educated than someone in their twenties, as well as intelligent, and only forty-two. No need to light a terrifying fire on the stove to cook the soup, no need to think and fight the urge to kill someone. Nothing. How quiet and calm it would be. And everyone around would feel pity for me, bring flowers to my grave and say what a nice person I was. *Had been.*

The desire to end this nightmare of a life was so strong that I looked for a place to land, without bushes or trees, soft grass or sand. Heaven forbid, I didn't want to stay alive and crippled forever. At that moment, I was not even thinking about any physical pain. My emotional pain was so strong that my brain blocked out every reason that could stop me. I found a place, the perfect place to jump.

And right then, Zhenia came home. Of course, we discussed all the wedding preparations. And of course, I didn't remember anything we talked about. My brain was on autopilot. Only one thought was in my head: to end up the conversation ASAP, and get rid of this hell inside. Soon, I told myself, I will hurry to my death.

Suddenly a thought struck me: Oh, my Lord! Vova! What about my son? I clearly saw the picture: I'm lying in a coffin, quite happy and relaxed, and my son is standing next to it, covering his eyes, for a man cannot cry. His mother taught so. And he is hiding his face for the shame, that his mother was so weak and had betrayed him, forcing him now to stand and bear this shame before all the world.

At such times, it is hard to expect from yourself even a tiny little bit of logic. My head was a mess and confused. I felt hot. So hot, as if a fire was burning me from the inside.

After we finished talking, I ran home. It's not an exaggeration. I ran as fast as I could. And each time that I stopped for breath, I almost turned back to do what I was thinking about, could not stop myself from thinking about. When I finally made it home, I poured myself a glass of vodka. Full. Then plunked myself to the foot of the couch and emptied another glass of vodka at one gulp. I felt no taste, no alcoholic content. After that I passed out.

In the morning my usual heartache and desire to end it all was mixed with a terrible headache and booze breath. But I didn't pay attention to anything and again ran. I ran to the same hospital where I was once treated for vegetative-vascular dystonia and migraine, the result of this very dystonia.

I was lucky again. The doctor on duty was understanding, and I didn't have to explain very much to him. After only a few words, he realized instantly why I had appeared in his hospital. He admitted me at once.

Chapter Fifteen

I stayed an entire month at the hospital. I had two weeks of treatment and strict restriction to the hospital and grounds, then two more weeks of much more pleasant therapy, along with a relative freedom of movement about the city.

I was lucky to have such good doctors. Perhaps it was only my personal impression, but I couldn't help but notice that Dr. Bagreev was a well-built, muscular man. One could say the same about his character. Even his jokes were too direct and strong. But no one took offense.

There was a remarkable woman with me in the ward. I had no idea why Valentina was here medically, but she was the owner of a very unusual and rare surname: Netahata, a name out of Ukrainian legend. The one that means that the bearer of the name isn't living in their own home. Actually, in the sense that those of the family Netahata have toys in the attic.

After I found out about this unfortunate last name, I decided to give a little moral support to the woman.

"Don't worry, Valentina, soon you'll get married and will finally be able to change your last name to a normal one."

"Oh, I am married," said Valentina serenly.

"Really? Then why didn't you keep your maiden name?"

"Well, my maiden name was also Netahata."

"That cannot be!"

"That's right, Polina. All my youth I dreamed of getting married one day, just so I could change my name," Valentina said. "Then I met a guy right in our own village. Fell in love with him without asking for the family name first."

"Who would have thought!"

"You know there are a lot of Ukrainian villages where one last name dominates. In some there are a lot of Ponamarenkos. In others, it's Kotsiuba. In our village there are several families with the last name of Netahata."

"*Hmmm*," I could only mumble.

Our kind Dr. Bagreev always cracked jokes about that name of Valentina's.

"So, Valentina, still not that *hata*? It's okay. Soon we will heal you and your *hata* will become the right one. Then you could change your last name to Tahata, the Correct House!"

Valentina was ready to take offense, and the doctor knew he was in hot water.

Bagreev saw a jar of pickled cucumbers on the table and said, "Ah, pickled cucumbers! All we need is a glass of bathtub vodka and a nice fat piece of salo–the perfect combination!"

"I will call my mom, she will bring everything immediately!" Valentina mouthed in pure Ukrainian and with the strong accent specific to her village.

We all laughed together.

———

On the day of my discharge, Dr. Bagreev invited me into his office and said, "Sit down and listen."

Dr. Bagreev was sitting at the table and doing nothing just looked at the paperwork. A minute. Two. I start wondering: Does he going to speak? Then he got up. Gathered folders that were there in a pile and put them on the edge of the table. He didn't look at me but walked through the room to window. Then he start talking. Quietly, slowly and surely, like a bud was talking to himself.

This all seemed very familiar. But I sat down and listened.

"I have been working as a psychiatrist for nearly thirty years. During my rather extensive practice, I've had more than a hundred cases of people who decided to commit suicide, thus to solve their accumulated problems, or to get rid of their pain. Some of them survived, but mostly they didn't. As a doctor, I know that at such moments, solving those horrible problems and getting rid of the mental or physical pain looks like the sweetest candy; the achievement of the most cherished dream.

"The human brain can lose, for a short time, the most powerful feeling in the world, the instinct of self-preservation. Only a very strong person, I repeat, *only* a very strong person can find the strength to resist this temptation and ask for help.

"The greatest complication is the realization that you cannot cope with this by yourself. Understand and accept this fact. You have to find the strength to ask for help, to confess your weakness. So you should know, my dear, that only really strong people can accomplish such a feat."

At this moment, apparently, a doubt reflected on my face because Bagreev repeated, "Yes, yes. For a person in such a situation, this is a feat. In my practice I've had only three cases like this. One of them is yours."

I stared at him with my eyes wide open, and listening as if his voice was the voice of an angel. Something in my soul started growing and strengthening. Something was changing.

"And now I'm going to tell you the most important thing of all. Listen, my dear, and never forget what I tell you. You are strong. You are beautiful. You are a smart and dauntless woman. And if you are able to overcome this, you'll be able to overcome everything, and achieve anything you want in your life."

He leaned over the desk toward me. "Do you understand? *Anything*." And then he sat down behind his desk and looked at me.

This man, so rigorous? and so kind at the same time, Doctor Bagreev, settled a feeling of strength and confidence in me. The belief that I was strong, that I could do anything, and would be able to achieve all my desires and dreams.

And things started to work out.

Chapter Sixteen

My first task was to get rid of my obsessive hatred. I thought about Maria Vasilievna and her supernatural, as it seemed to me, gift. I remembered the stories of people and how they were saved by the church and faith in God. So I decided to go to church.

Truth be told, as long as people are happy they are not in a hurry to turn to God. They live their lives, not always saintly, and sometimes expiate their sins with good deeds and thoughts.

But when you get into a difficult situation, start having problems with health, or worse, get sick with something incurable, that's when you begin to look for God. For this people tend to go to church. Where else? Only there you can atone for your sins, get help and hear God's voice.

I looked for salvation there also. But God and church? They are not the same thing. I do not want to offend any religious people who go to various churches and find comfort there. Moreover, many of them can't even imagine their lives without church and the people with whom they pray. And very often such people are connected with each other by something much deeper and intimate than belonging to the same Act of Contrition.

I'd been to this particular church before, looked at the icons framed in gold, lit candles for health and for peace. But never had I been so lonely and undeserving as I was now. All the recent events ached in my heart and soul.

I was told for a start, to make a confession so the priest could grant me absolution and bless me in order that I could begin to lead a saintly life.

As a supplicant should, I went to the church early in the morning, without having breakfast, and partook of the entire service.

For my confession, the priest asked me to come close to him, very close. He pushed my shoulders, making me lean over, so that my nose was almost touching his porky belly, and covered me with his vestments. Then he put the Bible on my head. He asked me about something and I answered automatically, could not even hear what, exactly. Hunger had sharpened my sense of smell, and the smell from underneath his robe was so terrible that the only thing I could think of was to get out from under it so I could breathe. Then he gave me a cross to kiss, a cross that had been kissed before me by everyone who came for confession.

So I didn't experience, I did not feel the main thing which made me go there to that church, that the Lord had forgiven my sins. I would say, on the contrary, I felt humiliated and unworthy of forgiveness, though my thoughts and soul must have been in full repentance. I never visited this church again.

The second attempt was spontaneous. My friend's father had died and I was helping with the funeral. After the funeral, we went with her to the church for the funeral service and the sealing. With us we brought everything required: some dirt from the grave, bread, eggs, wine, money, and a dozen handkerchiefs.

A woman from the church told us to put everything on the table prepared for the ritual. We had to wait for the priest. Meanwhile, another family arrived for the sealing of their deceased loved one. They probably did not have enough handkerchiefs, so the seller of icons and crosses came from behind her desk, took our handkerchiefs, and started selling them to the newcomers.

The next church I went to shocked me with its cheerfulness. The church members were singing and dancing on the stage, captivating everyone around with rhythm and their good mood. They were stomping their feet and clapping their hands, which didn't correspond to my inner state. So I realized that I had to cope with all the pain inside of me without a church, and perhaps even without God's help.

Chapter Seventeen

B ut I couldn't have managed without His help. One day I decided to visit my friend with the beautiful name, Svetlana. Svetlana always inspired me with her strength of mind, hard work, and constant desire to improve something in the interior of her apartment. She got married when she already had a daughter, Marina, and her new husband had two children from his previous marriage. His first wife was sick, and after her death, his children got a new mom, Marina for a little sister and another brother, Andrei, who was born soon after the wedding.

It was a mystery to me how Svetlana was managing to raise four children. Anton, her husband, was working a lot, and the children, household, a dog, and a cat were Svetlana's duty. She even managed to earn some extra money by knitting. She had a real talent for that, so there was always a demand for her work. Only Heaven knew exactly how she survived.

They lived in a small two-bedroom apartment near the city center. I still can't understand how all of them fit in it. I always dropped by to see her when something went wrong in my life. Seeing she was always busy as a bee but never lost her good mood and strength of spirit, I would come back home ashamed. I would think, This woman has a life much harder than mine, but never complains, unlike me, and other thoughts like that.

And now, years later, nothing had changed in Svetlana's life. Her daughter, Marina, went to work in London, leaving two daughters to be raised by their grandma. Apparently, my friend did not now have enough of her own resources, so she joined a church community. After learning about my situation, she invited me to go to church with her, and I did not dare to offend her by my refusal.

"Polina, I want to introduce you to our pastor, Vladislav Petrovich. Tell him everything, and he is sure to help you."

I smiled ironically at heart, but didn't want to show my real attitude to the questions of religion and church.

Vladislav Petrovich was, to my surprise, an ordinary man with an ugly, but not repulsive appearance, dressed in an ordinary suit. Even in his eyes, which are supposed to be the windows of his soul, I saw nothing special. It was only when he started talking I realized he was a priest with a God-given talent. His voice, a deep, soft baritone, penetrated deep inside and settled comfortably in my brain.

"Hello, Polina" he said.

"Hello."

"Tell me about your doubts, Polina, and I'll try to help you make the right decision."

I liked the fact that he did not offer to help me cope with my problems. I had already realized by this time that each person had to handle his or her problems independently. Apparently, my face reflected surprise because Vladislav Petrovich smiled gently and said, "Many people are waiting for God to solve all their problems. My task is to explain what's really going on and help them make the right decisions. I don't need to explain that to you. You already know that."

I was even more surprised.

"Why do you think so?" I asked.

"I don't think. I know."

Oh, I am lucky to meet the people in the know, I thought, and said, "Svetlana brought me here, and I did not want to offend her, so I came. After so many years of atheistic communist education, many people tried to return to a life of faith. I also tried. I visited various parishes in search of the path to God. Unfortunately, after all my attempts I feel nothing but disappointment."

"Do you believe that He really exists?"

"Previously I did, but now I am not sure. But I do not want to go to a church. I feel too uncomfortable there."

Vladislav Petrovich approached to me and looked at my eyes. Carefuly. I do not know what he was going to see there, but he, suddenly, smiled and shook his head affirmatively. I wondered what would it mean?

"For an exemple", he said, "If you need money, and you want to borrow it on your father, you don't need to go to your neighbor and ask him to do that. You can go directly to your father and ask him, can't you?"

"Well, in general, yes."

"And some can't. They can be shy, or just feel better in a company." And then it hit me.

"So you're saying I do not have to go to church? That I can turn to Him directly with my gratitude or for the help and advice I need?"

"Yes." Vladislav Petrovich smiled. "That's what I'm trying to say. God knows how to read our hearts. Moreover, he created us each different. Yes, in His own likeness, but different. Someone needs to go to church, to be among people. You have a different case. That is not by accident. God has plans for everyone. You're not an exception."

I was struck by the fact that the priest was not agitating for me to go to his church, to bring a tithe and sing prayers.

"What are His plans for me?"

"I do not know, I'm not God. But I have to give you some important advice. You must find strength to forgive the person or people who did this to you."

"How do you know?" I was surprised. "Did Svetlana tell you?"

"No. I do not know. Just my experience. You came here."

"But I came with Svetlana, not by myself."

"But you did come. Tell me, don't worry," his voice insisted and fascinated at the same time.

And I told him everything. I just could not resist the temptation to complain, to unload. But Vladislav Petrovich was a great listener. He didn't interrupt. Sympathy and outrage reflected on his face, depending on the nature of the narrative.

And then he said, "You poor thing. How could you live all this time with so much hatred and???? love! You should go to your ex-husband, bring him a gift, something he loved when you were living together, and say out loud the words of forgiveness. Out loud, do you understand?"

"What's the difference, aloud or not," I was angry. "I can't forgive him. I just can't."

"Did you try?" His voice became gentle and cushioned as an Angora scarf, making you warm on a winter evening.

"No."

"So how do you know you can't?"

I walked away with a determined desire to try. I wanted to do as Vladislav Petrovich advised me to, but just the same I determined my conviction that I couldn't forgive.

And only a fragile hope flickered somewhere inside, somewhere in my head or in my heart: what if? What if I manage to get rid of this pain, anger, hatred and self-pity?

Chapter Eighteen

That same evening, in order to not to put off this hard decision, or most likely I would change my mind, I called Aleksei. "Hi."

"Hi," he said, after a rather long pause.

"Can we meet? I need to talk to you."

For a moment he didn't say anything.

"Sure." Suddenly he agreed. "Only, come see me in my flat. I can't..." His voice trailed off.

I was surprised at how easily he agreed and how weak his voice was. "Tell me where."

I found the address easily. It was the mouse's flat. He had rented it while waiting for the money from the sale of our house. The Marina-mouse had left and moved to Israel. Without him. But that fact was less shocking than the way Aleksei looked. He was obviously ill. Extremely thin, just a set of bones, all pale and toothless.

I immediately recollected his old joke: "I have only two teeth, and they are not against each other." People have to think about what they say, even if it's just a joke. [where did he say this?]

Looking at my ex, I realized that he was very close to the point after which came complete silence. And again, it was as though my son was in front of me. And I knew that I could forgive Aleksei. I knew that Vova would suffer much if he lost his father. And I also thought that he would blame me for his father's death. Perhaps that's exactly what the wise Maria Vasilievna and Vladislav Petrovich were trying to tell me. I felt sorry for everyone: my son who could lose his father; my ex, because he was definitely in pain now, afraid, and certainly regretting what he did; and me, because of all the Hell I had gone through.

It reminded me of the suitcase of roses.

Vova and I were celebrating our birthdays. In fact, he was actually born the day before my own birthday. The doctor who was delivering my son offered to change the date on the birth certificate to one day forward, like mine, but I demurred. I already knew that the day, month, and year of birth made a difference in the life of each person. And I did not want to create confusion in my son's fate from the earliest days of his life.???? Destiny.

So we were celebrating our birthdays together in the middle of September. I was having my twenty-fifth one, Vova, his third.

The table was set. Guests gathered. Aleksei was late and I was angry. He had gone to visit his mother in the village. I loved my mother-in-law and never dissuaded him from visiting her, on the contrary, I believed that he should do it more often. But today, I thought he could have stayed home and helped me get ready for the celebration.

Finally the doorbell rang.???? why would ring his own doorbell? Aleksei came in with a medium-sized suitcase in his hand. Surprised, I was ready to hurry him up, when he opened the suitcase. The suitcase was full of roses. Red, pink, and white. Fresh, fragrant roses.

"Oh!" The guests uttered a chorus of *oohs* and *aahs*.

"Happy birthday, darling!"

How much I loved him then!

Now he was looking at me with the eyes of an old, tired, and beaten dog. There was fear. And suffering. And a plea.

"I brought tea," I forced myself to speak, holding back the tears. "Should I make the tea now?"

"Yes, please."

"I also brought some cookies."

"I'm forbidden to eat cookies."

"What has happened to you? You love cookies."

"I have diabetes. The acute type. My pancreas is failing. So..."

He couldn't say a word more. Neither could I.

I poured us some tea. I didn't put out the cookies.

"You know," I said after a while, "I've come to talk to you. I forgive you for everything you did. I forgive you."

Alexei's hand shook the tea in the cup.

"I forgive you, because we were together for almost seventeen years. Because we are responsible for our son, and because I thought about revenge. And forgive me if I have ever hurt you."

I did it! I did it!

But I was puzzled by the fact that he did not say anything. He was not surprised. He didn't say it was not him who had done it, or that it was me who made him do that. I realized that he was truly sorry for what he had done. For the fact that it was he, nobody else, who had tried to kill me. He just sat there with his eyes on the floor, completely silent.

Good heavens, you were so right, Maria Vasilievna! I didn't want him to be sick. I didn't want to put him to jail, nothing of the kind! Moreover, no prison could help a person experience remorse for what he did.

You were also correct, Vladislav Petrovich. I forgave him. I didn't want him to die. And the all-consuming hatred left me. Compassion came instead, and a sense of freedom I had not expected.

I was ready to cry from happiness. No, not because my almost-murderer was punished far too much, even for me. I did not want to punish him! I felt sorry for him. Sincerely sorry. I had the feeling that all this time I had been carrying a huge bag filled with something very unpleasant and heavy. And now it was gone. So easy to move! Such freedom!

We talked about various things, looking back on some good events in our life. Yes, there were some. In every family there are hard times and happy moments. And we were no exception. I thought back then that there was no woman happier than me in the whole world. And now I felt the same way.

Out on the street, I was close to tying my leg to that old, vanished weight because otherwise I felt I might fly away, like Piglet's green balloon. Wow! An idea flashed through my mind, how thoughts can physically put pressure on the body. I never would have thought that.

But now I didn't want to think at all.

The world around was so colorful and it seemed that before I watched it through a dirty window. Now someone had washed it for me, and everything around sparkled. Was it Someone or had I washed it myself? No, I would not think about anything. I was so happy! So happy!

Chapter Nineteen

Freedom from that obsessive hatred and the feeling of ultimate happiness instantly affected the quality of my life. I looked around and noticed things I had not paid attention to, probably since my romantic youth.

Look! There was a cloud resembling a huge, golden daisy. And this clean spring air fragrant with young greenery and lilacs! Even our hectic buses and cars, coughing up their fumes, could not kill the scent of spring and love.

I love it, I thought. I love everything and everyone. I love this girl who is walking with her mother, holding her hand and constantly asking some kid's questions, and the mother is answering with a tender smile on her lips. I love the guy, inputting something for ten minutes on his phone, and then all of a sudden either angry, or believing that the call will be faster and more useful, he is putting the phone to his ear, shouting, "Hey, hey! Can you hear me?" I even love that skinny croaker, with a face that expresses contempt for the whole world. Poor thing, she must be terribly miserable if she has such a mark of dissatisfaction on her face. And here a shoot of violets is making its way through the thickness of the asphalt and is about to flower.

Wow, I thought, so small, so tender, so seemingly weak, and it made its way through the incredible thickness of the asphalt to live. Live, perhaps quite a short life, because it can easily be ripped off by someone's evil hand or trodden down by someone's careless feet. But still it risks all that. It wants to live!

And suddenly I realized how much I want to live! How much I love life!

Chapter Twenty

Again, I am dreaming. This is not the usual city I'd been to previously. It's my apartment. I am home, watching television. There is something on the screen not too interesting, not too sad, just something you watch to kill time. The doorbell rings. I slowly get up and go to open to door.

I open the door and freeze, startled: there is a dog standing on my doorstep. My black dog that saved me from death in my last dream. My guardian angel. He came to me in a dream again. He came back to me!

He looked exhausted to a frazzle. His fur was dingy and ragged. He didn't look at me. He wasn't happy. I could not move. Tears were rolling down my cheeks, but I couldn't wipe them off, so they were dripping onto the floor. I was not sure why he came, so I was too scared to say anything. But he figured it out. Our guardian angels know everything about us and can easily see what we really think. Pushing me away with his snout, he walked wearily into the apartment, lay down on the carpet, and closed his eyes. I ran up to him, started hugging him, kissing him. Where was he all this time? What had he gone through? How did he survive?

What did he feel for me, contempt, hatred? Why was he back? Was he ordered to come back? Was it his duty?

Or was it his own desire?

I was crying out of pity for him, and out of happiness. He came back to me! I asked for forgiveness and promised that never, ever I would allow him to suffer because of me. It seemed he smiled gently to me, licked my nose and...

And, I woke up. I woke up in tears. With a wet nose and a clear feeling that I had just been licked there. And then I realized that he had come back to me. My guardian angel returned because he loved me, because I'd changed. Getting rid of hatred in my heart, I cleared a space for him, so that he could get comfortable. He came back to help. He returned to suffer for my mistakes and enjoy my right decisions. I did everything right. Thank you, kind Maria Vasilievna. Thank you, Dr. Dmitrii Nikolaievich, and wonderful Bagreev. Thank you, Pastor Viacheslav Petrovich. I am grateful for my salvation, for your lessons, help, and faith. I thank you all for the return of my angel!

Every person at birth gets an angel, a guardian. They accompany us through life. They bear responsibility for our actions. They can't solve our problems, but can whisper clues to solving these by a quiet voice of conscience. Some people hear that voice loud and clear. Others don't hear it at all. Or they don't like what they hear. They don't want to hear it. Such people have killed their guardian angels and live without them, believing that they know what's best. Are they right? I don't know. I think we are also responsible for our guardian angels. Everything happening to them depends on how we live, how we treat ourselves and others. And that's what defines us as humans.

I don't think my guardian angel actually looks like a Russian Borzoi. These angels know how to read our hearts and minds and assume the similitude of someone or something who is close to our understanding.

I got out from the bed and, taking a pillow and a blanket, I lay down on the floor, right on the spot where I had just been crying in a dream over my angel, exhausted by my mistakes. Closing my eyes, I could feel the warmth from something soft and woolly. I mentally embraced it and fell into a balmy sleep, so peaceful, and more relieved than I had felt for the last five years.

Part Two

Walking Down
the Aisle

S eptember. Indian summer. A warm, soft Indian summer. I
feel much the same as the air. Soft and warm. I understand, of
course, that the summer is over, but my soul enjoys this unusual
downy tranquility and the unity of mood and weather. These
September days the weather is always great. Even if it has rained
the day before, and it has been cold, by the middle of September
the weather always comes back to sunny, but not too hot. Warm
and calm with the charm of the autumn colors in their bright-
ness. Like a woman of forty, perhaps charming as never before
and never after. Beautiful, with that confident magnificence that
comes before fading. Just like nature at this time of year.

No argument there, every time of the year has its
own charm.

Spring is the awakening of youth, freshness. Of gentle, innocent, but exuberant flowering. The air full of viridity, bursting
with life and love. Thoughts and ambitions rush together in brassy
meltwater streams. Storming hormones. The time of conception
and development. The time of love.

During hot, zippy summer you want life in all of its aspects. It
seems that life has just begun. The energy of flowering is raging
with irrepressible passion. So good! Already strong, but still young
nature requires Life. So many more plans ahead! And here are
the pledges of spring love. Young, green and fresh. It's still spring
in their souls. Summer is the season of love, but???? consciously
deep and spiritual.

And then suddenly--what is this?

Fall? So soon? Oh, no! This is summer, but only the Indian one. And in your head you realize that it's autumn, but deep inside you try to catch and hold tightly to this designation, given by some tradition—Indian Summer. And after, blossoming with that particular autumnal splendor, you begin to persuade yourself that no, life is not coming to its end. Look how beautiful I am! And the desire to live is so strong.

And to love. Perhaps love is even stronger than in spring. It does not matter that the beauty is quietly falling down with golden and crimson leaves to the ground. But the pledges of spring love have grown up and matured. Now it's summer for them. And we try to stick closer together in order to feel the waning summer warmth. This gives us chance to postpone breaking, unprepared, into the severity of winter. They remind us that it is still possible to enjoy the beauty of the autumn.

So am I enjoying my autumn, though I understand that cold, frightening winter is just around the corner. It will come, as always with frosts, blizzards, and terrifying howls of the wind. It will come with lines of wrinkles, diseases, and weakness. It will cover us with silver-gray hair. It will end up in death. But that's not today. Today it is still autumn. September. Indian Summer.

Chapter One

Today was my fortieth birthday. The beginning of my Indian summer. We were celebrating it together with Natalia. It was still the same village and the same problem of selling the house and paying half the money to my ex-husband.

No words could describe my bad mood. Yesterday was my son's birthday. He was having his spring. He was eighteen. Eighteen! Once I gave myself the best present in the world—my son. Since then we always celebrated our birthdays together. But this year, the first time in his life, I was alone. He was having his military-student life, and I was so far away from him, and had nothing to please him with. No gift to charm him.

I'd had not much work. Even less money. Of course he received a small gift with a card and some money from me, and I was hoping that it would improve his mood. But it was unbearably sad to think that he had to grow up so soon. That his eighteenth birthday he was celebrating far from his family, surrounded by responsible, serious officers and dedicated fellow students. But there was nothing I could do, so I kept struggling, telling myself it was meant to be like this, everything will be okay.

I had no idea what was on the birthday table of my son, or even if he'd celebrated. On my table there was a bowl of boiled new potatoes, sprinkled with fresh dill. Pickled cucumbers, sliced and beautifully plated sausages, cheese, and a half-empty bottle of bathtub gin. Good bathtub gin. It was quite a modest birthday table.

Everything, except the vegetables and one gift, a book of recipes, were brought by my friend. One of those who were there in response to my need. She knew that I had neither money nor energy or desire to celebrate my birthday. In addition, the week before, I broke up with a boyfriend I was relying on to some extent. No, I didn't want to get married. To anyone. At all. Never! I'd had my piece-of-being-married-pie. But I desperately wanted to find a man with whom I would feel like a real woman.

My previous marriage, though it had seemed happy, in the end collapsed and nearly cost me my life. I had been married for seventeen years. Seventeen years of my life flushed into the toilet! On the other hand, there had been a lot of good moments. The best of them was my son.

Nevertheless I was sure I didn't want any marriage stuff anymore.

Anyway, I tried not to lose heart. Having got out of depression after the injury and its consequences, I learned to look at life philosophically.

But not one of my friends called or congratulated me. Well. Busy people. Or maybe they were just not real friends. Simply acquaintances. But Natalia came! My friend. And we needed nobody else. Not a very elaborate birthday table? Perfect for us. How much did we need, the two of us? We had bathtub gin. And not from a bad batch. This was made by Natalia's mom, with love and the best ingredients.

What a great mom you have, Natalia, I thought.

Broke up with a boyfriend? That means he never loved me. I would find a better one. That creepy man in Uman had told me I would be loved, happy, and rich. Could I have been happy with that guy, my former boyfriend? Too haughty he was. Puffed up all the time with his importance, vain as a peacock. One thing was good with him—he knew how to court a woman. Oh, and in bed, of course. So what if I had liked him? I would get over him. How could anyone like such a peacock?

In my opinion men were born to bring trouble.

Natalia's life was also not cloudless; she had rain on her parade. Though not a Hollywood beauty, she was a charming woman with a good body. Her wavy, medium length hair flowed over her shoulders, with a few gray hairs already, which didn't spoil her, on the contrary, even added some distinctive flavor. Big blue eyes made her look very beautiful. They say eyes are the mirrors of the soul. I thought that was not always true, but Natalia's eyes spoke sympathy and kindness. And that's how she was. Kind and sympathetic.

Her husband, Boris, with whom Natasha now lived in a common law marriage, liked to wet his whistle from time to time. They had been married for nine years and raised two sons. Then he found another woman. So they divorced. His new marriage failed, because he could never give his new wife what she asked for. Not to mention his drinking problems. So in the end, he came back to my friend. And she, without pausing to think, took him back. After all, he was the father of her boys. And boys needed a father. Any man was better than no man in the house.

He did not earn a lot of money, and even that was spent easily and quickly for booze. She was working as a nurse in oncological hospital, so her life could be called anything but easy.

The 1990s. A hellacious page in our history books.

People wrote it into the history of the countries of the former Soviet Union as the years of 'epidemic' trade and re-sell of things from Turkey or Odessa. Natasha went to bye things for re-selling to Odessa. She doesn't have enough of money to go to Turkey.

Then all things they bought there people re-sell on the local market. Due to have place in the market people have to pay for the place. Then they mast pay to "protectors", people who had nothing to do with "protection". It was clear racketeering.

So in the end almost nothing was left. But even with almost nothing she managed to save, and her husband immediately found what to spend it on. And she, good soul, gave away all her savings to him. The boys grew up and didn't want to continue with their education, so both were looking for jobs. Of course, none of the good positions required them, young boys without higher education. So my Natalia supported all of them. But she never lost heart, and even with all her problems, managed to help me. All this flashed through my mind as we were slicing cheese and sausage.

My poor thing. Such a kind and wonderful friend. I am so grateful you are with me, that you haven't forgotten me. You've come.

And me, exhausted with forced unemployment and the lack of money, health problems, and the constant squabbles with neighbors who still strove to chop off pieces of my land, I still felt happy. My angel had returned to me. My friend was nearby. My son was studying.

Though it was hard for him there, he was constantly supervised and directed. He was safe. So everything was going to be fine. I even had a real birthday party. With guests and toasts. Well, only one guest, but the most welcome one.

"So, Polina! Down the hatch. To your birthday. For your Indian summer!" Natalia raised her glass.

"Thank you, my friend. Down the hatch!"

"And now, one more to your health!"

"The third one for love."

We kept toasting and drinking. Then we danced, and then drank again. Then again. More dancing, only this time on the table. We were playing around heartily.

When we switched to tea, Natalia became sad. Her eyes were glistening.

"Why are you sad, Natalia?"

"I feel so sorry for you." Suddenly she burst into tears. "Are we in the middle of a desert? You've helped so many people. Where are they all now? And your recent peacock? He could at least have called!" Now she was sobbing.

"Oh, my dear Natalia, don't be sad. Imagine us, things will be so beautiful. Five years from now, you will earn a lot of money... " I started dreaming, and raised my eyes to the sky.

"And your hair-cutting business will grow," Natalia said. She also rolled her enormous blue eyes in dreamy ecstasy.

"You will get a promotion." I continued to dream. "You'll be the senior nurse in your department. No, in the entire hospital!"

"Wow, that's too much, Polina. Head nurse of the whole hospital! To become the senior nurse in the hospital, I'll need some cosmic pull." My girlfriend laughed.

"Even just while dreaming? You should always ask for more, so at least some of the things will come true," I said.

"Well, in that case, you will sell the house, and buy a fashionable three-bedroom apartment. Even better would be a house. A huge, two-storied manor."

"Boris will quit drinking and will pull up his socks like a man and get a job," I said.

"You'll get married to a rich and good man."

"Again, this marriage nonsense!" I chided her.

A thought rushed into my head. "Oh, Natalia, where have you seen a wealthy, yet a good man here?" Despite my cynicism about marriage, I laughed.

"Well, then, maybe it will be not a local. A Frenchman or an American," my friend interjected.

I burst out laughing. "French? American? Come on! Why would they come here? Have you seen any around lately? They are in France and America. And even if by some miracle they come here, such an old trout, as I am, is the last thing they want. They are looking for young and beautiful fish. Anyway, when you become rich, you can buy a car. Do you want a car?"

"You bet I do. Don't want to carry those heavy bags from the market by myself all the time." Natalia sighed.

"What kind of car do you want?"

"A Lada. That would be cheaper to repair if it breaks down."

"I would like a Honda," I continued my dreaming. "Or a Mazda."

"My goodness, Polina, you want your bread buttered on both sides!"

"That's what dreams are for. They're all for free." I went on having fun with my wild, impossible desires.

"Let's have a toast to that. For dreams to come true!"

"Yes, yes. And dreams *always* come true, of course."

But still we drank a toast to that.

"Can you imagine, we could take our boys on vacations to Yalta, to the seaside? Or even to Sochi."

In the life situation we were in, Yalta and Sochi were the same as Venus or Mars. So remote, almost unimaginable. Just like all the things we dreamed of.

"We will buy beautiful dresses," Natalia prompted me. "And we'll walk along the tree-shaded avenues in big summer hats. Then we'll swim in the sea and sunbathe on pristine exotic beaches."

"And they will serve us fancy cocktails in beautiful crystal goblets from a silver tray."

"And then an American will approach with a polite 'How do you do?' and just over his shoulder we will see his gorgeous Cadillac."

"Yep. All shiny white. Oh, Natasha, you are a wild sort of dreamer." I laughed heartily. "Come back to earth. Come on, one more drink, the last, and then it's bedtime for us."

Then we were singing Russian folk songs, drunk from alcohol, sadness, and despair.

Surprisingly, we ended up enjoying every second of that evening. Natasha left the next morning for work, and I began to think how we could possibly realize all our plans. Well, if not all, then at least the first and the most important: to sell the house, pay my ex his part of it, and with the rest of the money, to buy a flat for myself.

Chapter Two

The solution, came unexpectedly and directly right to the house. A young couple was looking in the village for an affordable home for themselves and their two children. They did not have all the money needed to buy right away, so they liked my idea: they would give me the earnest money. With this money, I could pay all the debts for the house bills, and when they paid me the rest, we would sign over the property to them. So it was a deal.

For the completion of paperwork all the family members from both sides arrived. For the last time my ex tried to convince our son to give him his part of money from the sale of the house.

"No, Dad," said my eighteen-year-old grown-up boy, "We're men. We are stronger. Mom is a woman. I can't, I'm sorry.

"Mom," our son addressed me. "If I give you my portion, will you be able to buy an apartment and then pay for it?"

"Yes, of course, but it will be your apartment, too."

"Don't do that, Mom. You should be the only owner. For one person the bills will be half the cost."

"Thank you, my son," these the only words I could whisper, unable to continue from tears choking my throat. "Thank you, but you should know that it will be your home too."

For me it was strange to realize that this generous young man was my son, who grew up so fast in the last few years.

When he was leaving for the entrance exams at the military institution, he was not yet seventeen. We were putting him with Aleksei on the train and when the train was ready to leave, Vova told me, "Exams are from 20 to 28 of August. If I come home earlier, do not ask me anything. It means I failed. Okay?"

I knew he hated losing. I felt so sorry for him! Sorry that I couldn't go with him. Sorry that he was so young and had to leave home without any financial support. Sorry I had no money to pay for his dream, which was medical school.

He must have been so frightened. And sadness was filling each part of my lost soul. I came back home from the station, howling. It was a true howl of despair. As a she-dog losing her puppy. In full voice.

And then a warm and gentle breeze touched me. Something whispered in my ear, "Don't cry, don't cry, everything will be fine." Then the warmth covered my shoulders, and stroked me on the head.

"Is that you, my angel? Thank you." I even wanted to smile and to believe that everything would really turn out fine. And I believed him. I couldn't explain it but I did believe him.

Every morning I would go to work, and on returning my heart skipped a beat. Was the door open or closed? Oh, closed. So he was still there, still passing his exams. There was still some hope, some chance. I was praying. I tried to be strong, no matter how difficult it was.

I had to keep my hands busy. Cook. Clean up. Grub up weeds. Even if there was nothing to pull up. Watch TV, read a book. Just not to think. Not to worry. Not to be afraid. I prayed, Forgive me, God, for my fears. Help me, angel!

And again there was the feeling of light warm soft touch, "Everything will be fine. Everything will be fine."

That Saturday I was calm and confident that my son was doing well. There were still four more days before the end of exams. "He will pass them," I kept saying. "Everything will be fine." But as I was leaving the house early in the morning, I saw Vova entering our yard. A duffel was flung over his shoulder, the bag he had packed before leaving.

It's over. He failed, was the first thought I had before I fainted.

When I came back to my senses, I saw my son's face, a little worried, but at the same time happy.

"Mom, Mom! I'm all right. I passed! Don't worry, everything is fine," he said, and smiled.

Everything is fine, everything is fine. He did it! These thoughts were rushing in my head.

"You did it? But there are four more days of exams." This was the only thing I managed to mumble.

"I did it, Mom, I did them so fast! I passed the exams. I was accepted. They allowed me to come home till the first of September. And I'll have to bring money to donate for renovations of the rooms we are going to live in."

———

That was only a year ago, and today he was an adult, refusing to knuckle under and give his own money to his greedy father, and giving it to his mother for her own dwelling. I felt happy that I had such a generous son, and completely broken-hearted at the same time that I couldn't afford to refuse his offer.

"I'll buy an apartment and will pay for it, but you should know that it is your apartment too. Your home. And you are more than welcome, please... God bless you!" I said, and burst out crying.

Soon, by good fortune, I bought a small one-room apartment on the third, the prestigious, floor. Was it a sign of good luck?

My major problem with dwellings was solved.

Chapter Three

So, as they say, I started to live happily ever after. Busy with daily affairs, I didn't notice how a few more years passed. I was trying hard to figure out whether I was doing everything right, if I'd truly learnt the lessons taught me by my life. I was reading a lot. I was working a lot. So my barber's business and well being both kept slowly growing.

About this time Vova married a girl he had known since childhood, and they were expecting my grandchild to come into this world. I was happy, and truly loved my daughter-in-law. We lived in the same house with her family and watched our children growing up together and being friends.

Savoring the beauty of single life, I didn't miss marriage at all. But after five years of this, in October a life-changing event happened. Of course, at that time I had no idea how transformative it would be for my life.

The weather was strange. The air was filled with wet mist. It was not quite a fog, but not rain yet. There was no wind so this soggy mist seemed to seep into everyone who had the courage to go outside, and get deep under the skin. I had to go out for a meeting with another possible client so I off I went.

"Polina!" I heard a voice behind me.

Turning, I saw Veronika. She wasn't one of my close friends. But our city was so small. I knew Veronika due to my friend, Zhenia, who had advised me to read Mikhail Veller's novels. The persevering heroes of his story, saved by the ambulance doctor, Zviagin, helped me to make the correct decision at a critical moment, and not to take away my own life before its due time.

I was still in touch with Zhenia. Though she had quite a prestigious position in our local newspaper, it didn't prevent her from being a good friend to me, an officially unemployed woman with no great achievements in my life.

So Veronika, perhaps with this in her mind, said, "Hey, I'm going to meet Zhenia."

"Oh."

"How are you?"

I wondered if she really wanted to know how I am doing, or if this is just a formality, I thought. "Okay," I answered, unwilling to commit as to how I really felt.

"You don't look that good. You seem exhausted or something."

I think you'll agree with me that such a compliment can be said only by one woman to another. A man would lie or, at least, say nothing. Oh, Veronika!

She looked stunning. She was wearing a beautiful and very expensive leather coat of a nice deep wine color, with boots matching it, and a perfect hairstyle. My clothes could not compete with hers. A cheap quilted jacket, neat, but pretty shabby, old boots I'd used to work in my garden, and no hairstyle to speak of. Everything was bought at the local market, and not in an expensive boutique. But to my surprise and pleasure I noticed that I didn't care how elegantly Veronika was dressed. And I had no desire to look like her. Strange. This would not have happened five or six years before.

During this interior dialogue, a picture from my distant youth came to my mind. I recollected being in that central square of that provincial Uman city, walking with Liuda. Yes, that first beauty in the past, the one I wanted to look like. The one whom that strange man predicted would live with the Sword of Damocles hanging over her, because of her own daughter. I had met her recently, that very daughter? What has been happening with Veronika?

Chapter Four

"Polina?" A low, hoarse voice called me.

"Yes. Me. Hello."

The face of this tired old woman was definitely familiar, but I could not remember where from. And then, like a flash! "Liuda?"

"You don't recognize me?"

"No, I'm sorry, I was deep in thought and it took me a few seconds to come back to reality." I tried to turn it into a joke. "How are you, Liuda?"

"Well, as you can see..."

I really hadn't recognized her when she spoke, this exhausted old woman. I wanted to know more about her life and what destiny had forced to become like this.

"How are you?" I asked, trying not to show how surprised I was with her frayed condition.

Once, walking along in Uman city center, we met a man who had said a few words to each of us. This man, old as death itself, had never left my thoughts. Now the memory of that man was as clear as ever. "And you, your daughter is going to be your Damocles' sword," he had said, addressing Liuda.

"Let's go and have a cup of tea," I said, pointing to the lovely cafe across the road.

Liuda was hesitant.

"I'm buying."

The story, she told me over that cup of tea, knocked me dead.

"Do you remember," she began, "you and I went to the same school? During the last year I started dating Oleg Pshenichny."

"Oh yes! He was the king of the city!" I exclaimed without thinking. "Not surprising, then you were such a beauty!"

"That's the thing. I was."

"Well, you are still beautiful," I lied.

Liuda, ignoring my phony compliment, continued. "So, we got married. There was plenty of money, so life seemed perfect. We went to Turkey and Egypt for holidays, even to France. A year later our daughter was born."

Oh! A daughter! So the old man had known what would happen to Liuda thirty years ago. He knew! How could he know? And if he knew that, then maybe he was not simply an ugly old man! Who then, was he? Did that mean that my future was supposed to become better? Though I was predicted to have a happy and rich life, it was hard to believe in that, and for some reason, even scary.

"Do you have children, Polina?"

"Yes, a son."

"Well, then you know that at the beginning, especially the first year, a woman devotes herself to the child totally. So I did. Moreover, my Ira was such a sweetheart. Oleg loved her, of course, but did not help me. Even worse, he went on one bender after another.

"At first I would complain and argue with him, then I started going for an overnight at my mom's place, and finally, I filed for divorce. I have no idea how he arranged it, maybe with some of his money, but a week later we were divorced. Then, threatening to take away my daughter forever, he started taking her at first for just a few days, and later for a few months."

"And did he take care of her by himself?" I could not believe it. "He always thought only of himself."

"No, she lived with his mother. And that woman hated me."

It gave me the creeps. The farther into the forest, the thicker the trees.

"To cut it short, when Ira went out of control, the same as her father, they gave her back to me and never asked for her anymore."

"What happened to her? Where is she now?"

Evidently, it was hard for Liuda to talk about it, but on the other hand it seemed she needed to share her grief with someone.

"Well, Polina, she is in prison," Liuda said after a moment's pause. "For six years already. Another five years left. Better if she stays there! I am horrified to think of the day she will get out."

Liuda finally started eating her little cakes with her tea. I was also silent. The silence continued, and than I dared to ask, "What is she in prison for?"

"First, her friends were prostitutes. Then she started on the drugs. And then, then... Well, she killed her boyfriend, and also stabbed me. I somehow survived, but he, poor guy, didn't."

"Oh, my dear heaven!" I gasped.

"Such a good boy, he was. Ira is beautiful. He loved her, you know? He came to talk to me and wanted to help her. Do you understand? We were talking, when Ira, furious, ran into the room, with a knife in her hand, well, and..."

It was harder and harder for Liuda to continue. I realized that I needed to end this torture.

"Miss, could you bring us more of tho-o-ose cakes?" I changed the topic, turning to the waitress. Thank Heaven, it worked. Liuda seemed to calm down a bit. Perhaps she was resigned to her fate, or somehow just got used to it.

My reactions were difficult to describe. All my skin was covered with goose bumps and my body felt numb. I could not move, not a finger on my hand or a toe on my foot.

"How are you?" Liuda finally asked me, realizing she had to be polite and ask about my life.

But I couldn't tell her anything. First of all, I had no words for my life after what I had just found out, and secondly, I doubted she remembered me mentioning that old man and everything he told us. She hadn't even seen him there.

"Nothing special," I said, "like everyone else."

———

And now, talking to Veronika, that meeting with Liuda flashed in my head within a few seconds. "All is not gold that glitters," says one of our proverbs. And another is "Beauty is only skin deep."

So while I was thinking about this, Veronica kept talking. When I returned my mind to reality, I heard. "If you want, I can register you on a dating site. My husband helped me to open a dating agency, so that's my main business. I was just going to see Zhenia, to place the advertisement. Sure, your chances are low, well, because of your, you know, age." Veronica couldn't resist a sarcastic mention of that. "How old are you?"

"Forty-five."

I could almost see horror from such a high number reflecting on her face. However, coping with her emotions, she said, "Well, maybe some old rich man. You'll inherit all the money. The fee is only fifty *hrivnas* per month. And I will translate your letters and—"

"No, no! I don't need old men, or a rich man or a poor man. And I don't know the language, and it's too late to learn it! And I have a pregnant daughter-in-law; I'll have grandchildren soon! And I don't want to get married. Regardless to whom."

I had a lot of reasons to refuse, though only one was enough. I didn't want to get married.

"Well, it's up to you. Call me if you change your mind."

I will not, I assured myself. But out loud I said, "Say hi to Zhenia from me."

And we channeled off, each one on her own business.

———

If I gave a name to it, I would call what happened next the story of one day. Everything happened during that same day: the morning meeting with Veronika, and sending a letter to an unknown American possible-friend in the evening of that day. As regards that letter, I would find out about that in about a week. Seven days later.

As it turned out, Veronika shared her impressions of our meeting with Zhenia, once she crossed the threshold of her office.

"Can you imagine, I've just seen Polina! So weather-beaten," Veronika shared the obvious with her fellow critics. "So poor and miserable. I invited her to sign up on my website and look for a rich old man. And she refused! You see, she doesn't want an old man! Who does she think she is? The daughter of a millionaire? Women are so foolish. Forty-five already, and she still hopes for a young guy!"

Zhenia, a woman of patience, listened to her, and said, "Don't pay any attention to what she says. Here are some pictures we can use. It's Polina on my birthday. Register her, and in the meantime, I'll persuade her it for the best."

"Well, what about money? Who will pay? It's not for free."

"How much?"

"Only fifty per month. You know, our girls mostly don't speak the language, and I have to translate the letters from the Americans, write the answers in English or in German, if necessary." Veronika started advertising her skills.

"Yeah, for Polina that's not small money, but here's enough for the first month." Zhenia took out bills from her bag and handed them to Veronika. "Then she will pay for herself. I'll convince her."

Veronika, delighted by the unexpected income, rushed home, where she had a letter to translate. It was written by one of her American clients, Ken, to his fiancée, Oksana. The letter, of course, was in English, dated November 21.

Hi, dear Oksana. Alaska is already covered with snow. So our work is done. As I told you, me and the other guys are building roads. So when the snow comes, it is impossible to do anything. There is a man working with me who also wants to come to Ukraine and meet some nice woman. Do you have a girlfriend older than you (40-45) for my friend Mike? If you do, then ask her to write him, and send a picture. Here is his e-mail.

We've already mailed the documents to get our visas, so as soon as we get the passports and visas, we're buying tickets. I'm looking forward to meeting you, my dear Oksana. I loved your letter. Your English is getting better and better each time you write.

Ken

So Veronika, without any hesitation, sent my pictures which Zhenia gave her, along with a letter in which she painted an outline and my best qualities to an unknown American from distant cold Alaska. No, of course, if the letter was from a New York millionaire, Veronika would not have sent it. But for some truck drivers who were building roads, almost miles from nowhere, what did she have to lose?

Meanwhile, I had not a clue about all this.

Chapter Five

A week later, Zhenia called.

"Polina, I need to talk to you."

"What's wrong?" I got worried. Usually confidently loud, Zhenia's voice sounded surprisingly soft.

"Polinochka, my dear, remember, a week ago when you saw Veronika?"

"I do remember."

"You see, she was going to meet with me. And I had your pictures. Well, I gave her some of those and she received a letter..."

While she was telling me the whole story, my emotions went through the whole range of emotional coloring, starting with anger and confusion, ending with gaiety and interest.

"Well, what am I supposed to do now?" I asked, finally recovering from the surprise.

"They, the Americans, are coming in February. And it's not that big a deal. If you let him stay in your place, his name is Mike, you will be able to show him the city. Then Veronika said she would take you both to Kiev. You'll get a vacation, have some fun. After all, no one is forcing you to get married!"

That's true, I haven't had a normal vacation for eternity, I thought.

"You've been single for nearly ten years."

"Eight."

"Well, eight. Will anyone forbid you to date?"

"No one will!"

Was I single for so many years? No, I certainly had a boyfriend. And again I had once thought that there was no one better than him in the whole wide world. Only after he was no longer in need of my help in doing laundry for his elderly parent, he proved himself large as life and twice as ugly.

New Year's Eve was close, coming soon. I asked twenty times how and where we were going to celebrate it. I knew I was pushing, but we at least could discuss it.

"Well, you know, I have a father," was his answer.

"So? Will we celebrate at your place with him?"

Once again I tried to get a clear answer.

On December 31, in the afternoon, he knew exactly where and with whom he was going to celebrate the New Year.

"I'm leaving," said my boyfriend when I found him packing.

"What about me?"

"You are staying. Anyway, I never promised you anything."

That was one New Year's Eve I would never forget! Russian tradition has it that how you celebrate New Year's will dictate the course of the next twelve months. So I decided that to be dumped and hungry at the same time was clearly too much. I laid a magnificent New Year's table with an Olivier salad; you can't have New Year's Eve without it. And to the salad of potatoes and vegetables, I added a fine piece of smoked ham, and was lavish with the mayonnaise. I also had a bottle of champagne, and many other delicacies.

And when, at ten o'clock in the evening, I got a call from a good friend of mine, who asked to come by to give me his best wishes on the New Year's Eve holiday, and stayed till morning, I realized that I would be neither hungry nor alone during next year.

But on the second of January, my leaving-you-on New-Year's Eve-boyfriend returned with a bottle of champagne and box of chocolates, and as if nothing had happened, he exclaimed, "I missed you so much! Come on, give me a welcome kiss!"

"Don't come on to me! Just get the heck out of here!"

Proudly I held up my head, with a look of contempt to emphasize my attitude towards him. But that was not necessary. He was shocked: How was this little nobody standing up to him?

"What did you say?"

"You heard me! Get out of here." I pronounced each word separately and distinctly. "Should I tell you where exactly to go?"

"Did you, did you think twice before you said that?"

Ha! Did I think twice? I wasn't thinking at all. It burst out in anger. It's no joke to leave a woman on a New Year's Eve, and then come back, as if nothing happened and to demand love! My index finger was pointing to the door.

"The door is there."

"I am a free man!"

"Exactly!"

"And I never promised you anything," he tried to justify himself.

"Maybe you should have!"

"You," he continued, trying to worm his way back into my affection. "You can ask me anything. Just never ask for money. Well, that, or to marry you!"

Wasn't he charming?

I smiled. How you celebrate New Year's will dictate the course of the next twelve months.

I came back to the present. "There is no one who will forbid me, I am a free woman."

"Of course, you are!" Zhenia encouraged me.

"Okay, give me that Mike to meet."

"Veronika will call you, so tell her about yourself, okay?" Zhenia was delighted.

"Agreed."

Now I had to prepare my small flat to meet my dear new American friend.

Chapter Six

All the time before the arrival of the foreign guests I was trying to find more clients, more work, to get more money for little trifles to improve my apartment, and to make it more cozy and comfy. It was a little scary, but I was very curious. What were these Americans like?

During the Soviet era, which was a big part of all my childhood, adolescence, and adulthood, America was the embodiment of pure evil. Soviet propaganda didn't allow people even to think those rich Americans could be good people. Capitalists and bloodsuckers. If law-enforcement authorities found US dollar bills in your wallet or in the apartment, it could lead you straight to jail.

And I could not get my head wrapped around this: why did they live better than us, if they were so bad? Why was the USA such a powerful country? Why were retired Americans traveling around the world, while our retired people considered their life over? Why did a simple truck driver have enough money to fly to the opposite side of the globe from Alaska, 4731 air miles, all the way to Ukraine, to meet his virtual bride. Our drivers were barely making ends meet. So I thought it would be interesting to know the answers to all these questions.

Having found my school books in the English language, I began to recollect the learnt material. But there was nothing to recollect. Except for a few words from the curriculum, I remembered absolutely nothing, and therefore had to buy a Russian-English dictionary. The dictionary also didn't really help me to "recollect." So Veronika gave me a few lessons for additional fees, so I at least could address a person properly. And as for the rest I had to rely on her totally.

Veronika called me from time to time, and I read the letters of my virtual American friend. I told her about myself and she wrote to Mike in my name. Four months passed like this. During this time, I duly paid Veronika for services. Mike didn't write often, two or three times a month, but his letters were full of content and interesting to me. He described his way of life, beauty of the place he was living and working in, and his thoughts.

Finally, the day of the arrival of the Americans came. But just the day before, I decided it would be nice to do something with my hair. I took the last money I had and went to an expensive beauty parlor to do a haircut for me at least as good as that of Veronika. I explained that I was expecting a man to arrive from the States, and that I had to look like a lady. The venture spectacularly failed. Whether the stylist was not that qualified, or this was her strange idea of a style for a lady, or whether she was just jealous that an American guy was coming to me, not to her, anyway, she cut my hair so short that I looked like a teenage boy. And no combing and styling could save the situation.

Besides, Veronika didn't take me to the airport to welcome the guests. There was no room for me in the car. Oksana, who, of course, was going to meet Ken, took her fourteen- year-old daughter. So I waited at home and cooked a special dinner for our dear guests. And though it all was pretty exciting, my mood could hardly hold onto the level of satisfactory. I think you could understand why.

Finally, the doorbell rang. I opened the door and froze. On the threshold there was a group of people, headed by a man: tall, athletic, with a handsome face. I was particularly struck by his unusually nicely shaped nose, and big blue eyes that looked at me piercingly and coldly. B-r-r-r. I felt weird.

The second man was simpler, of medium height, quite strong, with longish, thin hair down to his neck. But his eyes were dark and kind. And he had a joyous smile on his face. Both were wearing baseball hats with an unknown word: PETERBILT.

I wondered which one was Mike. I hoped the one with kind eyes.

"Please, come in," I said a phrase learnt before today, with Veronika's help.

"Polina, this is Mike," Veronika introduced me to the man with the cold eyes, destroying all my hopes.

"Hello, Mike. My name is Polina," I said slowly, realizing it was perhaps the last phrase I could say in English.

"I'm Ken. Hi! It is so nice to meet you." Ken went on chattering, not realizing that besides Veronica and his friend Mike, nobody understood a single word.

I got depressed right away. Oksana was a young, bright blonde with long silky hair and red lipstick. The Marilyn Monroe type. And what American didn't love Marilyn Monroe? I might have had some chance to impress an easy touch like Ken, but with this tall handsome Mike my chances were equal to zero.

He, however, turned out to possess an extensive bald spot, but it didn't spoil his looks. On the contrary, the fact that he was not ashamed of it and didn't try to cover it up with the hair around it, inspired respect. For a man it's far more important what he has *in* his head than what's *on* it. This is my opinion, but I think that you will agree with me.

I couldn't understand my feelings. On the one hand I should have not cared, because I was not planning to marry either of them. But on the other hand, I had a strange, but strong desire for Mike to fall in love with me. What for? Well, was there ever any logic in a woman's feelings? Perhaps that was the reason. I was a woman. Realizing this, I became even more depressed.

Oksana and her daughter were at ease and relaxed, acting like the the hostesses, while I was sitting in my own apartment quiet as a mouse, just watching everyone eat the dinner I'd fixed. Gorgeous Veronika was talking to our guests, proud of her knowledge of English.

Oksana was stuffing herself with the red caviar she had brought. She was eating it with a spoon straight from the jar and then suddenly discovered that there was nothing left. "Oh, I ate it all! Well, you would not like it in any case." For some reason she decided this for everyone.

Oksana's daughter was paying a tribute to dinner with all the zeal of a teenage child. The men looked tired and confused. It was late, so Veronika, Ken, and Oksana with her daughter left for home. And I was left alone with a stranger from distant America. I was frightened. Uneasy.

After making a bed for him to sleep on my big sofa, I took my seat on the loveseat. Fortunately my guest fell asleep right away, as soon as his head touched the pillow. After washing the dishes, for a long time I sat in the kitchen drinking tea and thinking. Why the heck did I need all this? That the kind of person I was, constantly creating big troubles for myself, and then courageously overcoming them. But apparently, that was how the Lord created me. I didn't feel very grateful.

The morning didn't bring any improvement. Mike woke up at five o'clock in the morning, when I had just fallen asleep. The reason was clear: the difference in the time zones of Alaska and Ukraine was eleven hours. Meaning that when we had our night-time, they enjoyed the daylight, and vice versa.

I felt myself completely exhausted. I suspected that my guest was, too. Anyway, trying to remain a good hostess, I ignored my fatigue and red eyes, and treated my guest with coffee and fresh-fried pancakes made from dough with farm cheese, which he seemed to enjoy a lot. That gave me hope that not everything was lost. There is a reason one says that the way to a man's heart is through his stomach. It is said all over the world, I am sure. I was a good cook. I was curious as to what people were eating in America.

It turned out my guest was drinking coffee of very weak concentration, but in enormous quantity. And I'm not joking! During the first half of the day it was usual for him to drink one-and-a-half or two liters of coffee! To make it just so, I had to single out a special pan, and let him cook this tonic beverage to his own taste by himself. It was obvious that he was grateful for my intuitiveness, because in trying to explain it to me in words, he reached no success. We used gestures to express ourselves quite successfully, and soon we could more or less explain our desires. I think if anyone could have seen us, they would have cracked up laughing. Our famous clown and playwright-producer Slava Polunin could not compete.

The phrase book Mike had brought with him turned out to be very useful. Surely we were not the first to try to communicate without any knowledge of each other's language. So such a book was a big help. In general, it was evident that he had been preparing for this visit with me. He had read on the Internet all he could find about Ukraine. It broke the ice between us a bit.

Veronika called just before lunch. Before that, we had gone to a park, and done some grocery shopping. And by some sixth sense I guessed and showed responses to his uncomplicated questions, and we were quite at ease with each other.

Veronika then left us for three days to the mercies of Fate and only re-appeared just before the planned trip to Kiev. At first I went into panic. I was okay at dealing with Mike on my home territory, but what to do with him once we were in Kiev, I had no clue. How to express myself? How to behave? What to show him? What to cook? How to ask?

But Mike was patient and friendly and we both were probably ready for this next, big step. We had achieved three wonderful days in interesting conversations by means of the dictionary and phrase book, and walks around the city. I was grateful to Mike that he was not trying to hit on me or to share a bed with me. He was polite, attentive, and helpful. So by the time of our trip to Kiev, we had established a good friendly international relationship. I liked this mysterious American man. In addition, it was interesting to listen about life in America, so I decided to start learning English in order to correspond with him, and if things went well, I could go to the USA for a tour. I'd never thought about it before, but why not?

Chapter Seven

Kiev. A beautiful green city, where around almost every corner one can find something interesting. Here's Andriyivskyy Descent, the long winding street of cobblestones and the house where the famous writer Mikhail Bulgakov lived. He wrote *The Master and Margarita*, the story of good and evil that has been read around the world. Here was St. Volodymyr's Cathedral, with frescoes painted by the world-famous artists Mikhail Vrubel and Viktor Vasnetsov. Holy Sophia Cathedral, Saint Andrew's Church, St. Michael's Golden-Domed Monastery. Kiev Pechersk Lavra, the monastery that started out as a series of caves, and the Museum of the Great Patriotic War.

All this created a lasting impression on me, and Mike was just stoked on the beauty of the city, its historical and cultural heritage. I felt proud of my little Ukraine, and gratitude to this overseas man for his sincere interest in our history and culture.

There in Kiev, I introduced my American guest to my son. I was pleasantly surprised how quickly the men hit it off. Mike liked my son a lot; Vova liked Mike.

Oksana and Ken seemed not to get along well for some reason. She kept hinting to him that she needed him to buy something, many things, for her, and he, the silly, just did not understand those hints. Oksana was getting angry. Ken was getting perplexed.

Back home, Mike and I invited them for a dinner at my place. Mike decided to cook himself and please us with roasted pork ribs with barbecue sauce and baked potatoes as was traditional for his homeland.

Dinner was already on the table in my little kitchen, spreading an unusual, appetizing flavor all over my flat, when suddenly Oksana said, "Listen, Polina, let's switch our guys."

"What do you mean, switch?" I was surprised.

"Well, easily! I don't like Ken. I like Mike more. He's handsome. And I am beautiful too. A better match. And you, as I've understood, don't really care whom you sleep with. You're not going to get married. By the way, Ken is not that bad in bed. How's Mike?"

"I don't know, I haven't tried," I said sarcastically.

"At all?"

"At all."

"Foolish woman! You've just wasted your time! Or maybe you are just a stick-in-the-mud."

"Who told you I'm not going to get married?" I ignored her offensive tone.

"Veronika."

"Well, you know, I can change my mind." I seethed with indignation.

"Polina, when was the last time you looked in the mirror?" said Oksana with superiority in her voice, and laughed aloud.

It reminded me of something! Déjà vu, I thought, and then I totally lost control.

"Who the hell do you think you are, Oksana? Want to try for Mike? Be my guest! Do you really think every guy drools over your shape? Just bleach your hair white, put on that screaming red lipstick and you think it's done? Like that's all you need? Do not get too offended then if he doesn't want to experiment with you! What are you gonna do then? Huh? You won't end up with either of them. Go ahead, try it!"

"Oh, he will want me," said Oksana, and confidently paraded, wiggling her hips at Mike. Apparently, she was really confident in her irresistible body, platinum-blonde hair, and red lipstick. Mike was sitting at the table, ready to start dinner, when Oksana plopped down on his lap. Caught in surprise, Mike jumped up and Oksana with all the beauty she was ready to use a few minutes ago as her unfailing weapon, fell down *splat* on the floor.

As she fell, she grabbed the tablecloth, which was set with a steaming hot dinner. Cutlery, the bowl with hot baked potatoes, the pork ribs Mike had cooked according to a special American recipe, ketchup, all that with a crash ended up on Oksana's head.

"*Aarrgh!*" cried the temptress.

Ken rushed over to help Oksana get up, but then suddenly stopped, apparently realizing that something was not right in the way she had sat down on Mike's lap, and right in front of him. He turned to look at Mike, and Ken's expression could hardly be described. Something combining surprise, indignation, anger, and confusion. Mike's expression was no better. In addition to all the above-described feelings, his face reflected fear. Then all of us looked at Oksana, sitting on the floor and screaming wildly, and we cracked up. Loudly and uncontrollably.

The picture in front of us was so hilarious that we could not stop laughing. You know from school, if you have to be serious in the classroom, your mouth automatically stretches into an idiotic smile, and your body is shaken by stomach and throat spasms caused by the hidden laughter.

As ill luck would have it, Mike's special barbeque tomato sauce had spilled right onto Oksana's head and was slowly running down her face and her long blonde hair. Right on top of her head, like a small hat, there was a pork rib, slathered with the same sauce. In one hand she was holding a potato, probably caught in an attempt to save it from falling to the floor. Sitting there on the floor and crying, she looked like a large child. Only the expression on her face was not childish at all. It was awry with hatred and anger.

"What are you all laughing at?", Oksana screamed hysterically. "And you, you American pest, it seems funny?

Ken could not understand what she was saying, but he easily determined that her words referred to him, and that they were not nice or friendly.

"Polina, what did she say?"

"I didn't understand," I said, trying to calm things down after the hysterical laughter, even though I perfectly understood what the furious Oksana was screaming at him.

"You, you schemer! You set it all up on purpose, didn't you?" Oksana attacked me.

"Me? *Ha-ha-ha!* No, how could I? *Oh-ho-ho!* I had no way to know that you would try to get my man. *Ah-ha-ha-ha-ha.* Now, if I had known, then I would definitely have planned something like this."

"You are scum, all of you!" was Oksana's conclusion when she tried to get up. She shouldn't have done that. In getting up, she bumped into a side table. It fell down, and all the bottles of beer and vodka, the bowls of canned cucumbers and tomatoes broke into pieces on the floor. Anger and hatred are always bad counselors, let alone when it comes to romance, then it is necessary to be especially delicate. But Oksana didn't know that or was just overcome with her emotions. Whatever it was, she also lost this round in my favor.

I looked at Mike. He looked at his dinner, his hours of work destroyed, lying on the floor. Offended, he turned away and left the kitchen. I suggested to Oksana that she take a shower, and then I went after him.

"What was this all about?" asked Mike.

It was impossible to explain now what Oksana had wanted, and why it had happened. Using all my English vocabulary I convinced both men that tomorrow I would certainly explain all to Veronika, and she would translate, and offered to take them to a dinner at a nice restaurant.

After her shower, Oksana cooled down a bit, but the evening was still ruined. Anyone's attempt to smile she took as a personal offence. Ken kept badgering me as to why she wanted to sit down on Mike's lap. I diligently pretended not to understand what he was asking. Finally everyone went home.

The next morning, I called Veronika and explained everything to her. She translated to Mike, Mike talked to Ken, trying to turn everything to a joke. I had no idea that Ken believed in this joke version, but I didn't care, because Mike suddenly hugged me tightly and kissed me. Oh, it was a truly passionate kiss!

Chapter Eight

M ike and I spent another week talking, walking around the city and having dinner together. During this time, we met up with Ken and Oksana only once. I invited them to celebrate St. Valentine's Day in the office, where I was hosting the event. Their faces didn't look happy, unlike Mike's and mine.

Before the American men left, we decided to go out to dinner once again, for a farewell dinner. We chose a cozy restaurant with traditional Ukrainian cuisine, with waiters in traditional costumes and the appropriate interior decoration. Before that, after thorough thinking, I decided to study English, and if Mike didn't mind, to keep in touch with him. After all, even my grandmother could read and write in Polish and English, besides Russian. Why couldn't I?

I wasn't counting on anything more than a virtual friendship. But my unwillingness to get married was no longer that firm.

All of us were at this good-bye party. The gorgeous Veronika and her husband Vladimir, beautiful Oksana with the same expression of contempt fixed on her face. Mike and Ken were excited about the upcoming dinner and their departure. And I? I was a little confused, unable to figure out what I wanted more: for Mike to leave and for me to return to my normal life, or for him to stay, and for me to turn my calm and lonely life on its head, and live merrily and happily with my new American friend.

I couldn't say now who came up with the idea to determine which of the men could drink more, but I must say it was a bad idea. Everyone got drunk. Vladimir, accustomed to our vodka, was perfectly managing the amount of alcohol, but our guests were drunk as lords. Whatever that meant. At first Mike was trying to prove to me that he drank only once in a blue moon. But besides the word *blue*, I did not understand anything in that sentence.

But because I was drunk and knew for a fact that in Russian the adjective blue was used to describe a homosexual, I decided he was admitting to being gay. I was shocked, and immediately decided to end the relationship. Thank heaven Veronika noticed that I was about to make some stupid decision, and when I explained to her about everything I had supposedly realized, at first she laughed for a long time, and then explained that this expression meant rarely. There are months when the full moon appears in the sky twice a month. But this happens not very often. And that gave birth to this expression.

After this it was my turn to laugh. So after all, I decided not to jump to conclusions when I was drunk. Happy, I ran to hug Mike for not being gay.

Meanwhile Ken decided to get acquainted with all the diners of the restaurant. He sat at different tables, started up sociable conversation, then drank with them, ate, and even danced the *Hopak,* not worse than any Ukrainian.

At the end of the evening he stole toilet paper from the restaurant to take to America, show his friends and discuss with them the question: how could such a rigid paper touch such a delicate place as someone's bottom? So, we had a great time and enjoyed the evening to its fullest.

That night poor Mike was driving the porcelain bus in the john while I was sitting in the kitchen drinking tea and having no idea how to help him. Shame will never allow him to come to see me again. Those were my thoughts.

Next morning I was barely able to wake him up to get to the airport in time for his flight back to Alaska. But though it was evident that he was suffering from severe hangover, he acted normally, and even tried to joke when talking about our last night together.

Ken and Oksana were not talking to each other.

"Polina, did Mike give you any money?" she asked.

"No."

"At all?"

"At all. Why? Why would he"

"Ken gave me four hundred *hryvnas*, so I tore them up and threw them in his face."

"Why? After all, it's good money, almost $100. I could live for a month on that."

I did not want to talk to her. Not only because of a sleepless night, but in general, I was feeling down.

―――――

At the gate Mike said, "I left the book I was reading on the table. Inside I put a letter for you. I tried to write in simple words, but if you don't understand something, ask Veronika to help you. When you read it, you'll understand. Thank you for everything."

Well, that's it, I thought. He probably wrote that I was a good woman, and thanked me for everything, but we were too different and too far from each other. So it's the end of my adventure and happy time with Mike.

Back home, first thing I did was open the book. I found the letter and three hundred dollars that Mike had put between its pages. Considering the fact that it was possible to live for a hundred dollars per month, this sum was a fortune to me. The letter was easy for me to understand. I read without any difficulty:

"Dear Polina,

I spent two wonderful weeks with you. You are a very nice woman. I'd like to leave you some money as an investment in the development of our relationship. I suspect you would refuse to take it (I am sure you would), so I left it in the book, together with the letter. I would like you to find a good teacher who can help you learn English so that we could know each other better. I would like to return soon. Thank you for your hospitality. Mike."

I was grateful for the money, but the rest didn't sound too real. Time would tell, I decided, mentally patting my guardian angel on his warm, silky head.

After he came back into my life, I never lost him again, and from time to time, talked to him in my head, trying to figure out how to not hurt him again, and asked for help or advice. After this I lay down on the bed and immediately fell asleep like a baby.

Chapter Nine

Victor was a heaven-sent tutor. He had been teaching English at the local university in the department of foreign languages. Tired of the stupid rules of our educational system and various limitations on foreign language teaching methods, he gave up the work at the university and was now giving private lessons to children and adults like me. He had personalized and individual approaches to everyone, therefore the results were quick and evident. Mike wrote to me every day, called every week. And after a couple of months, I could understand him more or less and was even able to answer some questions.

I was studying hard. All the walls in my flat were covered with posters with words. Later on there were phrases I had to memorize. On the ceiling there was a huge poster, which contained neatly written irregular verbs in three columns. They also had to be learnt by heart. Waking up in the morning and opening my eyes the first thing I saw was this list of irregular verbs. The same when I went to bed. Willy-nilly, I couldn't help but read them twice a day, so soon remembered every one of them. And even when I was taking a bath, in the mirror, instead of myself I was looking at the lyrics that Victor asked me to learn at home. When I wrote an answer to Mike, I first showed it to Victor. He was checking not only grammar mistakes, but also the general sense of the letter.

Once, after reading my letter, he asked, "And what are you trying to say here?"

I explained.

"But you've written totally the opposite! In English, there can't be two negatives, the so-called double negation, because the denial of one denies the latter. As the result you get a positive statement."

That's how tricky the English language turned out to be.

But after he clearly explained my mistakes to me, we used to laugh at what Mike would have thought if he had read the letter the way I first wrote it.

Sometimes, even after thoroughly learning a given task at home, in the morning after getting to class, I discovered that I remembered absolutely nothing. That made me angry. I even cried a few times. Victor smiled silently, gave me the opportunity to cry out all the insecurity, and would explain the material again. So the time was going fast for me, doing my work, and being in English class.

Chapter Ten

The second half of April was particularly good because of its wonderful weather. Warm air, full of the delicious scent of flowering apricot and cherry trees, was tickling the nose, and increasing the content of adrenaline in the blood. I wanted to sing, dance, and enjoy life. I wanted to love. And it was not just me. Cats were screaming at night. Thank heaven I was not a cat, otherwise I would scream myself hoarse, I thought, and I laughed. But I was a human being and my system of self-regulation to fix myself up was working perfectly.

Self-regulation of mood became my primary target as soon as I got discharged from the hospital after the accident. I thought if the mere thought of a lemon could make salivary glands produce saliva, why not imagine yourself joyful, happy, and make your body produce those hormones responsible for good mood? It turned out you could! Of course, it didn't happen by itself. I had to learn how to do that, and I worked hard to succeed. The development of these abilities took me about two years. But what a wonderful result. The technique of this phenomenon is described in the books of many doctors, psychologists, and even in some fiction.

One of these techniques I learned from my former classmate, whom I once visited after surviving the explosion and burns. Having settled down in one of the most favorite places of Ukrainian women, the kitchen, we made some tea and plunged into a passionate discussion about the meaning of life and how to make this life more happy. Nina, the name of my classmate, was an artist. Most such people had a creative and very delicate soul. There was a total collapse and disorder in the country, and such delicate sorts, such as my Nina, suffered from deep imbalances that prevailed in almost everything. I was not one with a delicate nature, but I also suffered. So we both were looking for a way to happiness, or at least some spiritual comfort, conversing with pleasure on how to learn to be happy.

Until recent times it was believed that genes, education, and training built up a character, while character affected one's destiny. But then there began to appear different studies of scientists, doctors, and psychologists, which promoted the idea of Kozma Prutkov, Tolstoy's character who always said, "If you want to be happy, be happy."

Many philosophers and religious had already come to the conclusion that a thought is material. Now neuroscientists and physicists confirmed it. It turns out that we are able to create our own destiny. Or, at least, to dream, so that those dreams could be fulfilled. With a dream, a wish, or a prayer, which may create some sort of space in the cosmic ethers, which the universe rushes to fill in the shape of our thoughts.

One of the main conditions for fulfillment of one's desires is to be happy. First be thankful for everything that surrounds you, and therefore you'll be happy. And then you can dream and make plans for this dream to come true.

We were having a wonderful time over a cup of tea, discussing the questions of the universe, religion, pedagogy, and psychology, smoothly moving from one topic to another.

"Polina, I have an idea," suddenly said Nina, with a mischievous twinkle in her eyes. She was pretty sure in everything she was saying or doing, while I was still crammed with doubts and insecurities that any of these ethereal methods could work.

"What? You want me to make a wish, go into trance and fulfill it? I don't mind! I laughed.

"Well, something like that. I need you to come up with a desire and write it down on this paper. And then, from time to time, just look at it."

"Do I need to show it to you? Or anyone?"

"As you wish. Up to you. The main thing is that you truly want what you will write down now."

After such a productive dialogue I went home in high spirits, with a note in my pocket and words written on it: "I want five thousand dollars." Why five thousand you may ask. Well, I have no answer for that. Then I didn't really care how much I wrote down, because, well, there was no chance to get such money anyway. And a sum of five thousand dollars was something unreal and magical in my head. But, believe me, I absolutely sincerely wanted it.

Opening the door to my apartment that night, I heard the phone ringing. For some reason, my heart started beating much faster than usual, so I reached the phone in one leap, and grabbed the receiver.

"Hello, dear!"

"Oh, Michael!"

Mike was calling to tell me that he was arriving in three days to see me again. He wanted to help me get an international passport so he could invite me to Alaska!

I slowly sat down on the sofa. May be I would not need to get hoarse from loneliness. The mood became even more joyous. Oh, my gosh. When we were talking with Nina, I just thought that it would be nice if Mike came over again. I didn't say anything, but I thought it. Wow. Gratitude and love to the whole world covered me with warm soft waves. How beautiful this spring is! How wonderful it is to live! Why didn't I feel it before? And why did I start understanding it only now?

Chapter Eleven

S pring. The time of year when everything comes to life and renovates: nature, body, thoughts, and feelings. All insults and failures are forgotten in spring. In spring you begin to believe that if you start all over again, you'll succeed. And right next to me there was a man who knew how to make me feel young, strong, and beautiful.

Ten days of spring passed as it was lived all in one day. The spring air intoxicated me and forced my whole body to work for the sake of love. The streets, all covered in snowy-pink petals from flowering fruit trees, delighted Mike. Perhaps there, in Alaska, it was also very beautiful, but with some other kind of beauty. I would know for sure when I go there.

My English lessons had achieved great results. My American friend was knocked dead with my success. After all, only two months had passed since our last meeting. Then we couldn't do without a dictionary at all, and now we used it only occasionally. He tried to speak in short sentences slowly and distinctly. I tried to combine the familiar words in the meaningful sentences. We were happy as children when we managed to understand each other.

He told me a lot about himself and his life. He had three brothers: Ken, Don, and Ron. The latter two were twins. Mike was the oldest in his family. When the older boys were nine and seven, and the twins were only four, their mother died after an epidemic of hepatitis. In those days this terrible disease was fatal, or maybe, because of frequent childbirth she was weak or maybe it was God's will. But out of nine cases she was the only one to die. Mike's mother was only thirty-four.

Mike told me that he did not remember much of that period of his life. He just recollected that his mother's skin was very yellow, and he was very sorry for her. Once he hid behind the wooden barn and prayed, asking God to take him, Mike, instead.

"My goodness but you were only nine!" I exclaimed, unable to understand how such a little boy was willing to sacrifice his life.

"I felt sorry for my mom, my dad and especially my brothers. How would they grow up without a mother!"

"Didn't you feel sorry for yourself?" I couldn't stop wondering at such willingness in a nine-year-old kid to do this heroic deed.

"I wasn't thinking about myself. Anyway, I also couldn't imagine my life without my mom."

It was the last time Mike prayed. No one knew what was going on in his small but selfless head. Everyone was busy with adult stuff. His father's grief. His mother's funeral.

Mike's father was left all alone with four madcaps on his hands. We can only guess how hard it was, and how he was able to raise the kids. Grandparents on both sides helped at first, but later on he got a well-paid job in Alaska, and they left, all five, to conquer the cold far north. Listening to this story, I realized that I loved that self-sacrificing boy. I loved this man who was that boy, and I would try to do my best to return a faith in God to this man.

The visit was short. When he was leaving, Mike said, "It was strange to realize, but when I arrived home last time, I felt that I really missed you. I came back to check my feelings for you now. You can be sure I'll be back in autumn. I'll be back."

This time, I believed him.

Chapter Twelve

As time went on, life continued to make me happy. I had enough work to live, not rich, but comfortably. My son's own life-summer began. The time came when his son was to be born. My first grandson. During his birth, I was standing at the window of a labor ward, where I heard his first cry, announcing his arrival into this world!

Unfortunately, pregnancy left us with complications. Anna, my daughter-in-law, had been forbidden by doctors to get pregnant. She was very slim and weak, so on the advice of her mother she decided to hide the pregnancy even from Vova, and told him only at the sixteenth week of term. She just confronted all of us, including Vova, with an accomplished fact. For me it was much like a betrayal, but Vova loved this girl, and I was happy for him. Anyway I felt sorry for Anna and always tried to support her. Moreover that was my grandson!

But life didn't forgive betrayal. The punishment followed immediately. Bad pneumonia in the middle of the pregnancy challenged the birth of the kid. All the doctors we consulted with gave unpromising predictions: after so many antibiotics and extremely low hemoglobin, the child was unlikely to be born healthy. Only one woman, a professor with forty years of experience, gave me hope. At first she didn't even want to talk to me. She was angry.

"How could you allow your daughter get to this point! With such poor health, she shouldn't have gotten pregnant. I don't even want to talk to you!" The doctor turned away and headed towards the door.

"I am her mother-in-law."

The doctor stopped abruptly and looked back.

"What? Mother-in-law? But where is her mother?"

"Well, it's not that easy to explain. Her mother is very worried. She cannot be here. And I have to. I must support not only this girl, but also my son. Besides me, there is no one to support him. After all, it will become his responsibility, both moral and material, if this child is born.

Doctor looked at me with her eyes wide open. I closed mine to gather thoughts in my head, rubbed my forehead and continued, "*Mmmm*, unhealthy. You know what I mean? And not only for the child, but also for his wife. Everyone will feel sorry for her, but who will feel sorry for my son? There is only me to help him. You know, I have to help the kids make the right decision. So, please, help me."

"I would be careful giving them advice."

"No, no. The decision will be made only by them but I have to help, to provide them with information. What to expect, what to do. So what do you think?"

"Okay, let's talk." The doctor softened. After a long conversation she said, "Nature is wise. You can only pray and hope."

And I prayed. Not sure if it was correctly, but it was with all my heart.

I was standing near the window, on the other side of which there was a miracle about to happen. Only the Lord knows how scared I was. After a couple of minutes, when I heard the cry of a newborn, my phone rang in my pocket.

"Well, Polina Aleksieievna," I heard the doctor's voice, "congratulations on your grandson! What a nice and healthy boy."

"Thank you, doctor, thank you!"

I could feel the tears of happiness running down my cheeks. Thank You, God! A miracle happened! Such happiness in my heart!

"Thank You, God, a nice and healthy boy!" And I prayed silently, thank You, thank You. Please send him a good guardian angel, like You gave me. Thank You, thank You.

I immediately shared the good news with my son, who, by the sounds I heard in the phone, was also crying from happiness. And afterwards I called Mike. He was delighted with the news and the fact that I wanted to share it with him. So my son was starting his life's summer, while I, being in my Indian summer, was ready to enter spring together with my grandson.

Chapter Thirteen

Summer was a blessed time for weddings. I had a lot of clients. I continued to take English lessons, so now the phone conversations with Mike were more actual conversations than only his monologues.

In the evenings Natasha sometimes dropped by. We arranged girls' get-togethers, discussing current events and news from America.

"Oh, Polina! Mark my words, your Mike will soon come to marry you. And then we will find a nice husband for me."

"Sure, no problem. You are a good and kind-hearted woman, Natasha. Every man would be more than lucky to have such a wife. However, my marriage is still a big question. I have no idea what his plans are for our future."

"Uh-oh, I see now. You don't mind getting married, do you?"

"Yeah, I don't mind. Why not? He is obviously a good and kind man. He never lies."

Natasha knew my buzz-bug. Lies were unacceptable in any form. If I caught a man lying, that was a goodbye.

"How do you know he is not deceiving you? You haven't been there, haven't seen anything or anyone? How can you be sure?"

"Well, for example, I said to him once, You are such an interesting man, living alone for eighteen years. You must have had a lot of women."

"And what did he say to you?" My girlfriend laughed. "I suppose, something like, 'Oh, no you know, there were few or only one or something like that?'"

"No, he just said, 'Yeah, thousands of them lined up.'"

"Thousands?"

"I think here he fibbed a little, of course, but he did not pretend to be a saint, that's for sure. Moreover, he even told me a joke."

"A joke?"

"Yeah."

"A man comes to the store to buy a postcard for Valentine's Day, and asks, Do you have a card that says 'For the only one'?

'We do.

'Give me twenty-five of those.'"

"For sure, a man with a sense of with humor," Natasha said giggling. "And what did you reply?"

"Me? Nothing. What did it have to do with me?"

"Aren't you nervous?"

"Why should I be scared? He is there? I'm here!"

"And if he proposes, what's then?"

"Well, if he proposes, if he does that, then I'll start being scared/nervous," I replied, and we both laughed.

Chapter Fourteen

Mike did come back! [hugs kisses?]He arrived and immediately said, "I'm here for two months. I want to be with you a little longer to get to know you better, and for you to be sure that you can stand me longer than a week. Do you mind if I suggest we go somewhere, for example, to Egypt?"

"To Egypt? Of course I'd love to go! I've never been that far from home. Only you do realize I don't have the kind of money to pay for such a trip."

"Yes, I do realize this, so I'm offering you this trip as a gift. The costs are my problem. Moreover if I wanted to go to Egypt from the United States, it would cost me three times as much, because of the distances involved."

"Oh, then of course we will go!" I gladly accepted his offer. "I've never flown in a plane before. Is it scary? And where are we going to stay there? Is it true that the Red Sea is so salty that it's impossible to drown?"

Mike did not even try to answer my questions. He was just looking at me and smiling. Besides, I didn't need any answers. I'd get a chance to find them out by myself.

We were discussing the trip and solving the details that arose with its coming closer. Then, Mike showed me his ticket and said he would have to go back January 15th. Today was November 15th. Two full months of happy life and new experiences were waiting for me. My life was turning into a fairy tale. And every fairy tale has to have a happy ending. That was my thought at that moment.

"And what is the suit for?" I laughed, when I saw his neatly packed black three-piece suit.

"You never know." My friend blushed. "Anything can happen. For New Year's Eve, for example."

"Oh yes, I totally forgot." Soon we were to celebrate the New Year, 2005. And I would not be alone to meet it. And it was marvelous that I was finally with somebody, and who knew what might happen. But I didn't know, and the best part of that was, I had no desire to know. I stopped thinking about the future and devoted my attention entirely to preparing for a trip to a fairy tale straight out of the *Arabian Nights*.

Our flight was from Kiev, where we once again visited Vova and his family. My grandson had grown into a weak and willful child. He cried a lot, slept badly, and his poor parents were very tired. But that did not stop us from seeing them, and I noticed that between Mike and my son there began to be established warm relationships. This is a good sign, I thought. Despite that, I kept feeling some vague fear, like something bad was going to happen.

My Heavens! What if that old man from my distant youth was right? What if now my life will get better? What if this is the man who will love me?

I never forgot that old man from nowhere, who vanished the same way he appeared, and prophesied me a happy and rich future. In particular, I remembered him when everything was going bad. I comforted myself with the materialistic thought that there was no old man, that I had imagined the whole thing. And even if he had been real, there was no way to know what was waiting for us in the future. Totally incomprehensible and illogical feeling I had, the fear that he could have been right. If our common future with Mike brings only good to everyone, I started to ask, addressing Someone strong and powerful, then let it happen. But if someone, even one person, suffers from it then stop it now. Let nothing happen and everything remains as it is.

I was willing to sacrifice my own happiness for the sake of my son's or grandson's happiness. Sincerely and unconditionally. Was that right? I had to ask. "You, my guardian angel, you know what to do. Guide me."

Chapter Fifteen

Our vacation package to Egypt was booked for the end of December. Now it was the middle of November and Mike asked, "Can we go somewhere else till December comes? To the Crimea, for example? I heard from my friends that it's a wonderful place and there is a lot to see."

The Crimea, of course, was a nice place to visit in summer, and I loved going there in the off-peak season, when the sun wasn't burning the skin, the number of people on the beaches and in the city was much smaller and the price for food and hotels was falling, but I said nothing to change his mind. Dwelling and food prices were now probably even lower. And besides, I just wanted to travel, to see the world, and just take a break from everyday life and its problems.

The Crimea left Mike with the most pleasant impression. Mike, this friend of mine, an open and positive person, appreciated everything he saw with interest, and though he compared it all to Alaska, he was able to recognize the beauty and dignity of my country.

I was grateful to him for that and became more and more attracted to this stranger.

After visiting the Siege of Sevastopol panorama, Mike greatly surprised me, sharing his knowledge about the Crimean War in the middle of the Nineteenth Century, about the history when England and France united to oust Russia from the Balkan Peninsula and the Black Sea. As it turned out, the comedian Zadornov was wrong in his humorous stories, where he claimed that all Americans were stupid.

We both admired with great pleasure the rooms of the Vorontsov Palace, each of which was unique and individual, complete with exhibitions presented there, and a lovely park in which to walk.

But of the greatest interest for us was Livadia Palace, bought in 1834 by Count Lev Pototsky. Later it became the residence of the Emperor Alexander II, and Alexander III died there. Here the imperial family of Nicholas II spent their summers. In February 1945 Stalin, Roosevelt, and Churchill gathered here for the famous Yalta Conference.

Mike seemed to be glued to the pictures depicting this life-changing event and only very strong force could move him on through the exhibit.

Then there were the ruins of the ancient city Chersonesus, which was a Greek colony in 528-529 years BC, and the Modern Botanical Garden, fresh and fragrant. Everything was so unusual and new for my American guest. America counts only two hundred years of history, therefore the history of Ukraine with thousands of years shocked him. Mike was surprised with the antiquity of our culture, that we were trying to protect it, and were really proud of it.

The weather was cold as always in autumn, but that didn't stop us from visiting the world famous Swallow's Nest Italian restaurant in Gaspra, housed in a *chateau fantastique* built in 1912, and the extraordinary Glade of Fairy Tales in Yalta, filled with the wooden statues of characters from our fairy tales. There it was a big challenge to somehow explain to Mike who was who among those figures.

"Polina, and who is that?" Mike asked me, pointing to a statue with ears the size of its head, which stood next to the figure of a crocodile.

"That's Cheburashka."

"Who is the Cheburashka? Is that a bear cub, born in Chernobyl?"

"No! Chernobyl has nothing to do with him!" I burst out laughing. "It's just a toy. From a book. Imaginary one."

But Mike stubbornly saw a fat little bear cub with huge ears, even if not from Chernobyl. So for now I had to agree to "just a bear cub with big ears."

We were walking a lot, talking, laughing, and fooling around like kids. Mike turned out to be cheerful, inquisitive, and light on his feet.

"*Dushka*, look! And who is that?" asked Mike, pointing to the figure of Tiiani-tolkai, from a fairy tale about Dr. Aybolit, a veterinarian. It looks like an antelope, or a horse with two heads, and is a close friend of Dr. Aybolit, whose Russian name means "Dr. Oh-It-Hurts." At first I tried to explain who this imaginary animal was, which was also not an easy task, and then wondered, "Where did you hear this word, *dushka*?"

It turned out that Mike heard it in the bar car of the train, where we looked in for a dinner on our way here. There one of the drunken customers used it addressing a waitress. She didn't get offended, and even laughed, so Mike concluded that the word was good, remembered it, and decided I would be pleasantly surprised.

I was surprised, so he was extremely happy and pleased with himself.

Back home, in December we repacked our bags and went off to the land of legends and Pharaohs. To Egypt.

Chapter Sixteen

During my first airplane flight, I felt like it was the last day of my life. Of course I did my best not to display that, but after Mike showed the marks from my nails, which I dug into his hand every time we hit an air pocket, it would be foolish to persuade him I was brave and courageous. Moreover I was reassuring myself that everyone was scared the first time. But honestly speaking, I was very happy when the plane landed at the airport of Hurghada, where a guide, an unkempt Egyptian with a face only a mother could love, was waiting for us with his taxi.

He drove us to an unusually clean and beautiful five-star Hilton hotel. For me, an ordinary Ukrainian woman, struggling to make ends meet, strongly determined there was no way I could fall in love, not to mention get married, such a difference from my everyday life seemed like a miracle. Or maybe it was a miracle. My life was turning into a fairy tale. And I felt like beautiful Belle from my favorite American Walt Disney cartoon movie, *Beauty and the Beast*. Mike, however, didn't really fit the Beast's part, but for the Prince, transformed from that Beast, it fit him perfectly.

That evening we were standing on the balcony of the hotel and enjoying a starry sky.

"Do you know the name of constellation, looking like the Big Dipper?"

"Yeah, it's the Ursa Major."

"And do you know where the Minor one is?"

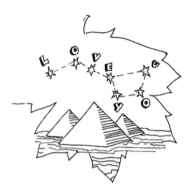

"Over there, the little dipper? And then, further the handle of the Big Dipper is the North Star. It must be very well visible in Alaska."

Mike was standing behind me and I could feel his warm breath. He gently took me by my shoulder, turned my face to him and hugged me. I clung to his strong body and felt that no one in this world could make us apart. Then he gently kissed me on the forehead, temple, lips.

"You know, lady, I love you..."

Chapter Seventeen

A chic hotel, gourmet food, a tour on the ancient Nile River with a few stops to visit the legendary temples built by the pharaohs of Egypt during thousands of years, extraordinary legends about love, power, and betrayal accompanying each of these temples. These were built in honor of the aspects of the many-sided God of the Sun, Ra, or other gods and pharaohs themselves. There were pyramids where pharaohs were buried together with their wives, servants, and wealth, and the Sphinx, whose nose was first shot off, not by troops of Napoleon as many believe, but by the order some zealot Mamluk in 1380 AD.

A declaration of love in an exotic land. Wasn't it all like a tale from *The Thousand and One Nights*?

Hospitable Egyptians were drumming up business, calling us into their shops, treating us to cold or hot hibiscus tea in the hopes that we'd buy something in their stores. In one of these, Mike and I went to get souvenirs for friends before leaving Egypt.

It was December 25. In a distant, unknown world American people were celebrating Christmas. We went shopping for souvenirs. In one of those stores, with millions of beautiful bottles of various shapes and sizes, hundreds of species which had been pressed into fragrant oils, Mike asked, "Polina, can you wait for me here, please? I need to go with the owner of the shop for ten minutes. This is his brother, Mahmed." Mike introduced me to another dark-skinned man in a long gray galabeya. "He will stay here with you."

Should tell you honestly, I got so scared that my hands went numb, my head went dizzy, and my stomach felt nauseous! This was it! Tomorrow morning we were supposed to fly home early. Here it was—the price of love. It was a trap for foolish, old, homely women such as me. He brought me here as goods, then he sold me and now was leaving me all alone without money or documents. He would fly away and these men would use me in all possible ways. I'd heard of many such cases.

God, I prayed, what was I supposed to do? Did I yet again get myself into a big mess? One I'd never get out of? He'd had a wonderful time, and now just wanted to get rid of me. Of course he sold me! It was my own fault. I had asked for it myself: "if someone suffers from it then stop it now." So there it was. Everything would stop. In my head the pictures appeared more and more horrible. Every minute I was expecting Mahmed himself or one of his co-conspirators to seize me, tie me up, or hit me. I stood, rocklike, in the middle of the store, unable to move. I was afraid that there were secret doors, which were plenty in number in pyramids all over this country.

And what did I expect? People told you, "look in the mirror!" I cursed myself up hill and down dale. An idiot! Lived long enough to get gray hair, but still naive as a kid! They say wisdom comes with age. But sometimes age comes alone. That was on the mark for me.

I mustered up my nerve. I had nothing to lose, for he that is born to be hanged shall never be drowned. Mahmed was sitting quietly at the table and drinking his tea. He invited me to join him, but afraid he might put some poison or sleeping pills in it, I refused. He did not insist. Minutes passed. Nothing was happening. I calmed down a bit. And then the shop owner came back with Mike. Happiness streamed from his face.

The shop owner was also smiling, and together with his brother they gave me kind, even admiring looks. Sizing up the situation, I decided never to tell anyone about the horrible ten minutes I'd experienced in the distant, foreign country of Egypt, standing alone in a small perfume shop. In fairy tales, terrible episodes happen also.

Mike came up to me, took my hand, and looked into my eyes.

"Are you cold?" he asked, seeing that I was trembling like an aspen leaf.

"Yes," I lied.

"Are you sick?" I could hear disturbance in his voice.

How could I think so badly of him? Again I began to curse myself. What else should I have thought? I don't know this man! It's really only the third time in my life I've seen him.

"I hope not," I replied. "Shall we?"

"Let's go."

We said goodbye to the Egyptian brothers and, hearing their congratulations when we were leaving, I thought that was for Christmas day. Mike kept my hand in his and was squeezing it tight.

"Here we are."

I looked up and saw SULTAN JEWELRY STORE. He probably wants to buy me some jewelry for Christmas, I thought. Well, perhaps, I should let him do that. After all, it was the third time we had spent some days together.

Chapter Eighteen

O ur world is infinitely changeable. I was just suspecting a man of the worst of crimes, human trafficking, and now was ready to accept an expensive gift and become obligated to him. But I still didn't know what destiny had prepared for me by introducing Mike into my life, and what obligation he was going to involve me in.

We went inside. It was a nice jewelry store, not too big, but respectable. Showcases, located on three sides, were shining with cleanliness, gold, and gemstones. Five Egyptian men, apparently salesmen, stood in a row, clapping their hands and shouting, "Welcome," "Congratulations," and "Merry Christmas." I, logically assuming that they were giving us their best wishes for Christmas, thanked and wished them Merry Christmas as well.

"Polina." Suddenly Mike turned to me. He took my hand and I felt that his hand was slightly trembling.

"Are you also cold?" I asked, jokingly.

He looked straight into my eyes. His expression was serious and he reminded me of that man I saw for the first time a year ago, to whom I opened the door of my apartment, his eyes cold and piercing.

"I want you to try on one ring and choose a second one, too."

"Two rings? Why two?" I was surprised.

He motioned my eyes to the counter with two rings lying on it. One was big, the second one was smaller. They were wedding rings.

"Oh!"

"I love you, Polina. Will you marry me?"

I froze on the spot. Even in fairy tales people often feel numb, I thought to myself. Suddenly I felt a strong headache and ringing in my ears. My body got stiff and refused to obey my wish that it relax. In just few moments, when I was able to move, I looked around at the men standing in a row. They were crying out, clapping, and laughing. It was obvious they were delighted.

Mike did not move either. He stood in front of me, staring into my eyes. His own eyes expressed suspense, mixed with doubt, and with something very tender as well. Why? I wondered. Why is he looking at me this way?

Something dripped on my hand. Dear heaven, those were tears. My tears, or his?

The men fell silent. Mike was waiting, while I was speechless.

I didn't know how much time had passed when finally I was able to whisper, "Yes."

A storm of applause and shouts of joy shook the Sultan Jewelry Store.

Did I say that? I thought, and said aloud, "I'm sorry. I was just not expecting that."

Tears were still running down my cheeks. I rubbed them off my face together with my make-up. Could you imagine what a beauty I was at that moment? My head was splitting from pain into thousands of pieces, and I had the feeling that I had stepped off a cliff. Directly into the deep unknown.

But Mike looked happy. He kept hugging, kissing, and embracing me.

"Please, Polina, choose one more ring, the engagement ring. Ali will show you where to choose."

Ali took me to the counter, where I saw many gold rings with little white stones. "So many beautiful rings with zirconium," I said, as I admired them.

"Can I have this one with three stones? It suits the wedding ring."

"Of course you can," Mike smiled somewhat mysteriously. "Now we have to wait until they adjust the size. It will take twenty to thirty minutes. We can stay here or walk around the local shops."

"Let's sit down here. This headache is killing me."

While we were waiting, I calmed down a bit and my sense of humor or something similar to it was coming back.

"Usually when a man proposes to a woman, flowers and champagne are the essential accessories," I quipped for some reason. Champagne? Why would I say that? Again I was chastising myself. Not long ago you were dying of fear in the perfume shop across the way, thinking that he had sold you into slavery! I was ashamed.

"I promise you champagne this night for dinner. And as for flowers, well, in America, if a man gives vegetables to a woman, then he can do without flowers."

"Vegetables? I'm lost."

"It's simple. Tell me, what measuring units are used for diamonds?"

"Carats."

And then it hit me.

"Carrots!" I laughed. And then realization hit me one more time.

"So those little white stones were dimonds?"

"Yes. They're diamonds," modestly replied my future husband.

"Oh, I'm sorry, Mike, for choosing a ring with three stones," I started making excuses. "I did not know they were diamonds. Can we change to another? No? What a shame."

"Why change?" Mike surprised. "It's a very beautiful ring."

"But it's too expensive," I murmured almost inaudibly.

But he still heard me.

"It's not an overly expensive ring. Take it easy."

But I couldn't take it easy, because in my understanding, diamonds were not something that could be "not overly expensive." But I said nothing else. Suddenly I felt very tired, not to mention the headache was still with me.

Chapter Nineteen

While I was sitting there in silence, Mike told me his plans for the wedding in the Ukraine as soon as we got back there. He wanted me to invite my son and his wife, relatives and friends, who, in his opinion, had become his friends, too.

That evening in the gorgeous restaurant at the Hilton, we celebrated our engagement. Early in the morning, we were sitting in the plane on our way home. Mike had his eyes closed, smiling, and holding my hand, on which a ring with three diamonds was sparkling, while I was thinking about the tricks of fortune.

How did it happen that, in barely half an hour, I'd lived a whole life? From humiliating and deadly fear in that little perfume shop up to the highest degree of happiness in the jewelry store across the road. How did it happen that during this half an hour I changed my principles and agreed to marry a man I didn't really know? A man I first suspected of betraying me and selling me to the slave trade, and then agreeing to spend with him the rest of my life in sorrow and joy. How did it happen that after living forty-five years of my life in one country, I would be able to see America, and maybe not just her? Oh my heavens, I was really going to leave my homeland, follow this man, and leave everything I had here. My son, grandson, friends, work, the very country itself! Did I trade all these for three little shiny stones?

Chapter Twenty

We returned home for New Year's Eve. Again, I thought about the tricks of fortune, all the reversals in a period of one year that seemed as long as a lifetime The previous New Year's Eve I was a miserable, abandoned, hurt, impoverished woman.

Today everything was almost obscenely contrary. I called my son.

"Hi, dear."

"Hello, Mom."

"Vova, Mike has proposed to me," I started right off the bat. "I said yes, but am very scared. Everything, however, can still be canceled."

"Mom! Come on! That's great! What are you afraid of? Why cancel? Mike is a good man."

"How do you know what kind of man he is?"

"I feel it."

That was true. Vova often "felt" people, especially when he was little. Some people could easily get his trust while others could not, neither for love nor money. When he began talking, sometimes, pointing to some of our guests, which were always in quantity in our home: "This is a good man. And this is a bad woman." And we also had the opportunity to find out that the kid was always right.

"And even more," Vova continued, "you are a young woman. You need to have your own life, because if you don't, you'll be like many mothers being a royal pain in the neck to their children. In this case, me. Of course, I will try to be a good son, but you know that would not be right."

I couldn't but agree with that. Some of my single female friends really could not find a better occupation than to be nuisances to their kids with their advice, illnesses, and problems.

One point for Mike. And an important one.

But I still had my doubts.

"But I'll have to go to America and leave you here. And little Vanya. Everyone will assume that I've betrayed my motherland."

"Oh, Mom. Why betrayed? Now the whole world opens its borders. People live where it's best for them, but not always where they were born. And what do you mean, betrayed? You're not selling the secrets of our country. You haven't stolen anything or killed anyone. You're just arranging your personal life."

Two points for Mike!

"And me, you're not abandoning me. I am an adult, a married man, capable of solving my own problems. After all, we do not see each other often, and you can call us from there, too."

Three points for Mike!

"And what if my life will not be good there and it won't work out?" I protested weakly.

"If it doesn't work out, you can always come back. This is not the Soviet Union anymore. Now people are free to move around the world."

Four points for Mike!

"What are you counting there, Mom?"

"Oh nothing! Thank you, dear."

So Mike won, and my son brought him the victory. That made me happy.

Chapter Twenty-One

I t's amazing how events can change us and our attitudes about the world. All of a sudden, from not that young a woman, exhausted with life, and constant troubles, you turn into the Queen of the Ball. Your soul is no longer tormented with doubts or any sense of insecurity. It lifts you up to the heavens, together with dreams, enjoying life, laughter, and cheers. Suddenly, how beautiful life is!

The usual room of the restaurant turns into a palace with white marble columns and exquisite dishes of exotic flavors. It is filled with flowers and music. You are surrounded by the crowd of people. They look at you with admiration, and some even with jealousy. Everyone is happy for you and say only nice things to you.

Life itself seems magical, especially if the event is happening on the eve of the old style New Year according to the Julian calendar. Nowadays it falls on January 14. This holiday itself is so incredibly dreamlike, that it intensifies this impression. And why? Because there is one man, the man who is now dancing with you, and looking at you with admiration and love. (His suit was more than necessary for this occasion.) For him also everything has changed overnight. He's received his prize. He's been looking for it. And now, finally, he has it in his hands a woman he wanted to become his wife. He looks at her as if she is the greatest treasure of the world.

Didn't you feel like that on your wedding day?

The next day Mike flew back to Alaska. To follow my husband I had to get a visa. For that I needed to provide a large set of documents and go through a number of procedures.

The holiday was over and my fears came back.

Oh God, what a coward I am! So, what to do now? What if he never comes back? Will I have to live with someone else's last name? I will not even be able to get a divorce, because of it being an international marriage. And what did I need all this for? Why couldn't I just live quietly like everyone else? But no, I decided to get married.

But these thoughts came to me less and less. I always felt the presence of my guardian angel. He seemed to be smiling at me and whispering, "Good job! You did the right thing. Everything will be fine." It gave me strength. I continued taking my English lessons and dreaming of a better future.

My husband also didn't give me any reason to worry. He called and wrote me letters. He was polite and kept me informed of all the issues concerning gathering the required papers. One of his calls was special.

"Hey, Polina!"

"Oh! Mike! Hi!"

"I've collected all the necessary documents," Mike said into the handset, "and will send them to you by special courier. I will have to leave for a business trip for three days, so I won't be able to write. You will have to meet the courier at the Borispol Airport in Kiev on Friday at two o'clock."

"And is this a man or a woman?" I felt nervous.

"I don't know," Mike said, "so you'll have to make a sign with your name on it in both English and Russian, so this person can easily find you in the airport."

"Okay, I'll do it," I said, and my heart filled with joy. He loved me. He hurried to take me to him.

Suddenly I recollected that during the dinner in honor of our engagement, when I expressed some doubts about his love for me, Mike said, "If you look at the globe, then you will see that your city, and Anchorage, the city in which I live, are at opposite sides of the Earth. This means that, coming to you and going back home, I make a full circle around the Earth."

"Well, generally, yes," I said, surprised that he even found out the location of our cities on the globe. I was stunned!

"So how many women do you know, for whom a man would fly the Earth around three times?"

Thinking about it this way, I admitted to myself that I personally didn't know any woman like that. Well, now, of course, I knew one.

Chapter Twenty-Two

On Friday, at two p.m. on the dot I was in Borispol Airport. In my hands I was holding a placard made of two album sheets. One album sheet seemed too small and therefore not reliable. On this poster, rather impressive in its size, in large block letters I wrote POLINA SMITH and Полина Смис. I was holding the pages proudly high above my head. It didn't bother me that no one else had such a big poster, as most people just took the sheets torn from a school notebook or notepad, with the name of the person written with a pen or pencil. People, were paying great attention to me and my placard. They came close, looking first at the names written, then at me, some smiling, some snickering, and then stepped aside. Sometimes I saw them pointing to me with their friends, as if I were a lunatic of some kind. I paid no attention to any of those, as my goal was not to miss the courier.

And then I saw him! He was passing through the gate, tired, but happy, smiling with such an innocent smile!

"Mike?"

My hands, holding the banner with my name, dropped down and my "art" fell on the floor with a great wallop.

"Miss, aren't you meeting a special courier with your documents?" he said.

"I, I am!" I twined my arms about his neck while my body was shaking with laughter. Tears of happiness were rolling down my cheeks and I thought, What a surprise! What a man!

When our mutual emotions piped down a bit, we were approached by a taxi driver, one of many in the airport looking for fares, who offered his services. We refused. But he was in no hurry to leave.

"Excuse me my curiosity," he said. "Tell me, whom were you meeting here?"

"My husband!" I said happily.

"You needed this huge poster to find your husband?" He was incredibly surprised, and went to tell other the taxi drivers about it. In five minutes I could hear friendly laughter from the drivers' crowd. In ten minutes, half of Borispol International Airport was laughing. An hour later, I thought, perhaps, all Kiev would be laughing.

Well, I thought as I smiled, let people have their fun.

Chapter Twenty-Three

The June heat was penetrating into the room and creeping into every corner it could reach. After exuberant spring blossoms, a warm, maybe even hot summer came.

Fresh, sporty and full of drive at the age of forty-five. These lyrics from a famous song kept twisting in my head. Stuck. I got angry. I hated that song. I preferred the songs of Soviet singer Valentina Tolkunova, with her music and lyrics so understanding of the feminine soul. I just couldn't stand the idea of being referred to as that kind of woman.

"You are forty-five and your life is just starting," sadly pronounced my friend Natalia.

"That would be nice." I was also depressed. "I have no idea what is waiting for me there."

It was hot in the kitchen, but not only from the warm summer air, but also from the oven, where I had just baked a delicious chicken with golden crust. A bottle of expensive brandy, champagne, fruit, chocolate—only the best things were on my table this time. A completely different class of goods than what I had for my birthday five years ago. Then we had fun. Now we were sad. It was a good-bye dinner with my close friend. Mike was full and went to the living room, while Natalia could not stop talking.

It seemed like I was flying to another planet populated with aliens unable to understand me, and me not able to understand them. Would I come back someday? Would I ever again see my children, grandchildren, and my friend?

This kitchen of five square meters? No. I would not miss this kitchen. I didn't want to see anyone else this last night before leaving Ukraine. No, of course I could have spent this evening with my son, but he was grown up and was living in Kiev and had his own family, his own life. We had said goodbye on the phone.

I was not even trying to pretend I was having fun. Natalia, as always, was sympathetic and positive.

"Everything will be fine. You get settled there and then we'll find me a date, maybe even a husband." She laughed.

"Yes, Mike said he had many single friends. If only Mike himself turns out to be the person he seems to appear."

"Polina, cut it out. If he'd wanted to deceive you, he would have introduced himself as a lawyer or doctor. They are more prestigious than some truck driver."

"Maybe, maybe."

Chapter Twenty-Four

The flight was difficult. Take-off. Landing. Again, take-off. Again landing, and again and again. Twenty-four hours like that. I couldn't sleep on the planes. Whether because of the fear or excitement, I didn't feel tired. Airports in Amsterdam, Seattle, and Chicago impressed me with their size and cleanliness.

For a while I forgot about everything, even about Ukraine, my kitchen, and friends. Life twirled me in a maelstrom of new events and adventures.

The first thing I realized when I landed in the United States was that during all the time I had been learning English, I learnt absolutely nothing. The alive speech of Americans merged into one huge sentence, from which I could not single out any familiar word. The one thing I could understand was "Welcome to the United States!" This phrase was said by everyone we had to face passing through Customs. They said that with sincere and joyful smiles on their faces. And it seemed to me that they were really glad that I came here! And even though we were both tired after such a long journey, my mood was wonderful. In general, America created a very nice impression on me.

It happened that three months prior to my arrival, Mike's grandfather died. He lived in Michigan and was ninety-four years old when he passed away. In the United States they prefer to cremate their deceased, so the funeral and the subsequent wake, the celebration of life as they call it, can be carried out at any convenient time. Moreover, there are no limits in timing for Americans like nine or forty days, as they are not so superstitious.

Mike's relatives knew that he was to bring his wife from the former Soviet Union and were eager to look at this miracle. Everyone was waiting for me! They, of course, believed that Mike again had got into just one more tough spot. Every time he tried to throw in his lot with a woman, it brought a lot of problems. The first time he married early, at nineteen, to a woman five years older than himself, who had two children. After divorcing her he was left, as they say, without a penny in his pocket.

His second wife was a friend and a kindred spirit. She was also a truck driver and loved to race on a snowmobile. They spent time together, hanging out in the bars, where she soon started hanging out more and more often. And not only with him. One day, when Mike came home from the night shift, he discovered that both sides of their bed were still warm from the heat of human bodies. Having decided that scandal couldn't be avoided, the traitoress left for a while. Later, she also tried to sue for some money, but my husband, sadder but wiser, took the necessary measures to prevent this from happening a second time.

So his family had reasonable grounds to believe that Mike again got into a jam.

All the relatives: brothers and their wives, aunts, uncles, cousins, who came to the celebration of life of the deceased grandfather, were smiling and friendly people. They also kept telling me "Welcome to the US," and "Glad to see you." And I again had the feeling that all these people would be very unhappy if I weren't here, so sincere they sounded. They all were so nice, I was happy.

The evening was coming to an end when I got surrounded by his brothers Ken, Don, and Ron. Mike at that time was having a conversation with someone else, and I, tired from the flights and sleepless nights, was sitting alone in the corner. The eldest of the brothers, Ken, said, "Polina! We have to tell you something very important. We have to warn you. We think you've made a big mistake by marrying Mike."

"Me? Why?" All my fears instantly flashed through my mind. Sticky, nasty, chillness crept up my back.

"He probably did not tell you, but he has five children here in the States. And after he went to prison, he even has a kind of a boyfriend."

"What? Mike in jail? Boyfriend?" I looked at them with my eyes wide. Perhaps there was so much fear in them that Don, the youngest of the brothers, gave me a wink. Ken, knowing his good heart, cut Don's desire to warn me by stepping hard on his foot. But it was too late. I realized it was a joke. To be honest, the guys disappointed me. Such a dodo of a woman, who came to a foreign country without knowing the language, the people, or traditions. It was too brutal. Three big guys were having fun looking at my scared eyes. It was a shame.

"I cannot answer you the way I would like to because of my poor English. So for now I will say this, as you are his brothers, and therefore mine too, you have to help me. Here I have no one else to ask for help. Can you refuse me?"

I saw sincere amazement on their faces.

"And one more thing. I advise you never to make such jokes anymore. You totally have no idea what a Ukrainian woman is capable of. If you try to offend her, she might strike back."

My impression of such nice people had been corrupted. Though not for all. Don was still a nice guy for me.

My husband came back happy and smiling. I didn't want to spoil his mood, so I told him nothing. Moreover I was afraid that he could find this joke hilarious too. I didn't. I was still scared that all of it, or at least part, was truth.

Chapter Twenty-Five

" My God! What is it? Is this your house?"

"This is *our* house!" Mike said, quite proud of himself. A rambler with wooden siding of a sordid yellow gray-brown color made me depressed.

The entire area in front of the house was covered with gray asphalt. There was not one plant or bush or tree. My eyes filled with tears. Do not panic, I said to myself. Maybe it will be better inside. He took me in his arms and carried me over the threshold.

"Welcome home!"

Oh, my God! How could anyone live here? The inside was even more depressing than the outside. A small kitchen, combined with a small living room. The same yellow-gray-brown tones, with a predominance of dark brown. The windows were decorated with ugly yellow curtains. A phone, looking like it was saved since the Soviet collectivization, was sitting on a table littered with papers and phone books. Nightmare!

Mike definitely had another opinion. His eyes were glowing with happiness. Looking at him, I thought, everything has its advantages. It feels like this place has never been touched by a woman's hand. Well, we'll see, I reassured myself.

Waking up in the morning, I immediately began the battle for my new life. My husband thought his life was fixed and comfortable, that I would just fit in smoothly and without any issues. I did not want to fit in. Besides the kitchen, combined with a living room, the house had two small bedrooms and a huge garage. One of the bedrooms, where his father used to live, and which Mike hadn't entered for two years, was swamped with old things, covered with dust. He was horrified when I started to take those things out.

"Don't touch it! It's my father's chair. He sat in it."

"This is my father's notebook, he wrote in it."

"This is my father's suit."

"And when did he put it on last time?" I asked.

"Three years ago," he replied.

Mike's father died two years ago, having grated on his nerves before. For some reason he didn't love his eldest son, whom he chose to live with after retirement, so he kept arguing with him, all the time living together. Before his death, he got seriously sick and their relationship became even more complicated. But, despite this, Mike spoke of his father with warmth and sadness.

"Okay, will you ever wear that suit?"

"No. It's too big."

"Then why is it here?"

"Just don't touch!"

I became depressed. I was feeling like that for three days, and getting prepared to go back home to Ukraine, I suddenly found a way of influencing my second half. An accident helped me. By lucky chance I came across a pretty immodest photo of my husband and another woman. The picture left not a single chance for any illusion about the nature of their relationship. It didn't affect me, I knew it was past. My husband was not a monk, and I was glad.

After thinking for a while, I decided to use it to start cleaning our house, minds, and souls of garbage from previous lives, and begin to build the foundation of a new life together, as they say, with a clean slate. I put this picture on Mike's bedside table. In the morning the photo was not there. Neither could I find it anywhere inside the house.

"You know, dear," I began to speak up my prepared speech. "It's good I found this picture now. If I found it a year later, I would never believe that it was done before we got together."

"What picture?" Mike blushed.

"Well, the one I put it on your bedside table, and now it's not there."

"I haven't seen any picture," he continued to lie.

"Oh, okay, but I still think you should give me chance to clean up our house, so you didn't have to lie like now. I promise I'm not going to throw away anything. I will simply hide things in boxes and put them where you say. I understand that you cherish the memory of your father, but for last two years you've never entered this room and never used any of these things. And something tells me you will not use them ever. Let's clean all of that nicely, and then make a study of this room."

"Good," my husband said, with sadness in his voice. "But do everything yourself. I can't."

"Okay," I was glad, finally getting the permission to act, though I tried to hide my joy.

The next morning I began my fight with old things, dust, and the feeling that no one had been living here for years.

I was putting things in boxes, mopping the floor, washing the windows, putting up the wallpaper.

And what's this? I thought, cleaning dust from the shelf of a built-in cabinet, when suddenly something heavy fell on my head.

"Oh!" I rubbed the injured forehead and looked at the floor in search of what it could be. It was a dirty, shabby envelope, stuffed with something.

"It hurts!" Again I rubbed my forehead. "What could that be, so heavy? Did he put stones there or what? Probably more photos." I was talking to myself. No one else to talk to while cleaning the house. But there were no pictures. It was money. One, two, three, four, forty-nine, fifty. Fifty C-notes. Exactly five thousand!

I could not believe it! Five thousand dollars fell on my head!

If it had happened to someone else, I would have never believed it. My eyes filled with tears, recollecting that night five years ago, when under the influence of my friend's convictions, just for fun I wrote on a piece of paper: "I want five thousand dollars to fall on my head!"

"It can't be happening," I kept saying to myself, "just impossible."

"It's good you found this, honey." Mike was glad for my discovery. "This was money I saved while working on the road construction in Kenai, and totally forgot about it for a while now. So, since *you* have found it, we will spend it on your training. You wanted to work as a hairdresser here, am I right? Tomorrow I'll sign you up in school."

Chapter Twenty-Six

My further life consisted of a series of achievements and successes, difficulties and disappointments. Difficult (because of my poor English), but quite successfully (though still had to take it in English) were my exams for a driving license, and Mike bought me a small, but very nice car, a two-door Saturn sedan. Sporty, maneuverable, and light, it served me faithfully for the next four years.

At beauty school, being the oldest student, I felt quite like a one-legged man at a butt-kicking contest. Mostly young girls of eighteen or twenty studied here. Not being English speaking, it was particularly difficult for me. But I tried. I tried hard. Teachers saw and appreciated that. Everything was fine, but not without small incidents. Of course, there was one person and, of course, it was a woman, a teacher-instructor, for whom I managed to stick in her gizzard.

"Polina, and how did you come to the United States?" she asked me once.

"I got married and my husband brought me here."

"You see, girls," she turned to all the female students. "These Russians take your men, and you sit here and let them do it with impunity."

What was she saying to them? Stupid woman. She didn't even remember I was from Ukraine, no matter that I had told her four times.

That evening at dinner, I told Mike this story, offended, and once again ready to go back to Ukraine. He calmed me down and taught me how and what to say if it happened again.

It didn't take long for her to try to upset me again. Pity you couldn't see her face and eyes full of anger, when I proudly raised my eyebrow and slowly answered, "My husband asked me to tell you that he can't speak for all American men, but he is sure that those who are going for their wives to Ukraine or Russia are not satisfied with the attitude of American women. That they should learn from such women, like me, otherwise in the near future all American men will travel to countries of the former Soviet Union for wives."

The owner of the school, having learnt about all this, soon fired this poor, bitter-at-the-whole-world woman instructor. Such an attitude towards students threatened the reputation of the school, and accordingly its financial wellbeing. *C'est la vie.*

Six months later, after successfully passing the exam, I started my professional path in the United States, a country I even didn't ever dream I would end up in.

A year after my arrival grief broke into our little family. Mike called me at school.

"Please, come home," he said, and I barely recognized his voice.

I don't remember how I got home. Fear paralyzed my mind and body. What happened? What could have happened?

Stepping out of the car, I ran to Mike, who was standing at the front door with such a sorrow on his face.

"I killed a woman," he said. "There was an accident."

"Oh, God! And you? Are you okay?"

"I'm not hurt."

"Mike, you couldn't. You couldn't kill her. I know how you drive the car. You couldn't! Tell me how everything happened."

The situation turned out to be more than common. Mike in his huge truck, a Peterbilt with a trailer, was turning left at the intersection of two streets. All his moves were perfected to the mechanism for years. He certainly—always—waited for a green arrow on the traffic light, which allowed movement for him.

On the perpendicular road a claret-colored Volvo was racing at the red lights. Without paying any attention to the car which was stopped in the other driving lane, nor to the red light, the Volvo, driven by a woman, crashed right into the middle of Mike's

36-foot-long trailer. My husband didn't even know what happened, so little was the impact from the collision felt in the cab. Nevertheless he stopped and approached the car, where he saw a woman, with extensive nose and mouth bleeding. Having dialed 911, Mike stayed there, waiting for the ambulance.

The woman died at the hospital. Mike was so shocked by the incident that now he wasn't sure if there *was* the green arrow permitting his turn at the traffic light. None of the witnesses of the accident stayed on the spot to testify to the police. It was the middle of the day and everyone was in a hurry.

The family of the deceased launched an accusatory campaign in the media. Everyone accused my husband. Only I knew that he wasn't guilty. He couldn't have begun turning without waiting for permission to move. Mike paced the room back and forth, like a wounded bear in a cage, and I followed him like a shadow everywhere. He was in such a condition that I was afraid he would do something to himself.

It was awful. Our life just began to settle. He was in love. And loved. And now threatened with jail? He was charged with involuntary manslaughter in the second-degree. I kept walking after him wherever he went, repeating like a broken record, "Everything will be fine. You couldn't have turned without the arrow. You'll see, they'll find out you waited for that green arrow. You'll certainly get free from any charges." It was only on the third day I managed to persuade him to eat a bit and sleep.

For a whole week the media was throwing the book at my poor husband. And then the first good news came from the police. There were witnesses. They called the police and told they saw a wine-colored Volvo, speeding against the traffic lights. Later police found out that the deceased had already been fined once for running a red light.

Having inspected the truck, the police had to admit that it was in excellent condition and worked properly. Thanks to heaven! We began to thaw out slowly. Until the investigation was over they made him give a written understanding not to leave the town. He was allowed to go to work, but Mike couldn't drive a car anymore. Each time he approached the car or the truck he got pale and perspiring. What to do? How to help him? He couldn't live without a car. Forty years behind the wheel! Oh, my Lord! Again, this magic number, forty.

Chapter Twenty-Seven

Bogged down in our trials, we didn't notice two weeks fly by. The pleasure from a Sunday morning coffee was interrupted by a phone. It was Pat, my husband's friend, who informed him that the snowmobile he ordered a month ago, arrived, and he could pick it up. It turned out my husband had bought me a snowmobile. Perhaps he also knew that it was better to buy one in summer. That was great!

On the one hand a snowmobile in July was, to put it mildly, neither here nor there, but on the other hand, I suddenly found in me this irrepressible craving for this type of transport and whined that I wanted to have my snowmobile here and now. I was even ready to drive if Mike was going with me on the passenger seat. So we settled on that, immediately packed up and went. Having passed a little more than halfway there, with longer than to go forward, I suddenly started complaining about a terrible headache.

"Oh, Mike. I can't drive any more, this headache is killing me. I feel dizzy, I just can't—"

He was silent. Biting the bullet, he got behind the wheel. I wasn't sure if he got my trick, but all the way to Homer, the city where my snowmobile was waiting, he drove in silence. Mike was pale and sweating. I pretended to be sick, though there was no need for that, as I was trembling from stress for my husband, and almost I cried with pity for him, but there was no other way.

Finally we safely reached Homer. Having loaded my snowmobile, over which I sighed and gasped for half an hour, either looking under the hood, as if I understood something in that, or in the bag for tools, expressing my admiration, we headed back home. My head was still "hurting," so Mike sat behind the wheel. Four hours of a journey, which he used to overcome in two. Five miles before Anchorage, Mike, gritting his teeth, passed a car for the first time since the Volvo had hit his trailer.

I sighed with relief. Thanks to God, he did it! Now everything will be all right, I thought.

There was our house. I felt like a boiled rag. Mike looked even worse: pale, his eyes glistening with some unusual light, his lips trembling. He slowly walked over to me and looked into my eyes. I thought, If he hit me right now, it will probably be right. But instead he dropped to his knees in front of me, embraced my legs, and whispered "Thank you."

Investigation of the accident took a full year. Finally the police sent us the report, in which the deceased woman was found guilty of the accident. Finally, our life could return to normal. Though how could it?

We had become different. We had changed.

Chapter Twenty-Eight

Increasingly, I began to wonder where my home was. Increasingly I caught myself thinking that when I was in Alaska, I missed everything I left in Ukraine. When I came to Ukraine, I wanted to go back to Alaska. How could that be? Why was I here? Of course, since I met Mike, life was good, but my mind was tortured by doubts and my heart was heavy. Though now there was no reason to doubt the prediction of that old man from my distant youth. I thought of him so often that he seemed to become my family. I always thought of him with some trepidation, fear, and at the same time with warmth and hope that he would be right. It turned out he was. Who was he, that strange old man? It seemed to me that I knew who he was, but my guesses seemed incredible. Tell me, who can know exactly what awaits us in the future? Only something as old as the universe itself, exhausted, but kind and wise—Life itself! My Life!

I had everything. I was loved, rich as I'd never dreamed of, but why did I feel so bad? And then, on St. Tatyana's Day, January twenty-fifth, I felt as sad as never before. Acting flakey, I yelled at Mike, stamped my feet, threw everything that came within easy reach. My terrified husband, ("What a monster have I married!"), tried to calm me down. My Lord! What am I doing? I thought, and ran out into the street, not forgetting to bang the front door loudly. An extraordinarily beautiful January was outside. Minus twenty-five Celsius. Everything was covered with thick, sparkling snow that was glowing somewhat unreal due to Christmas illumination on the houses around. But I didn't see the beauty of the winter evening, didn't feel the January frost. What is wrong with me? I thought. Where am I going? And more importantly, why?

I had nowhere to go and no reason for that. Crying, I was jogging in circles around the block. When I finally got exhausted from senseless running I calmed down a bit. I sat down on a park bench.

"God, please, help me," I prayed. "I have everything. Everything! A wonderful man, a warm house with plenty of food, clothing, jewelry, and a car. I have never lived so well. Teach me to be grateful to the man who gave me all of this, grateful to all that I have in my life, to life itself. Why is it so hard? Why doubts and uncertainty are eating me up inside? Where are you, my dear guardian angel? Tell me what to do? Where to get the strength?"

Tears were rolling down my cheeks, turning to ice the second they touched the ground. And then I saw my car, driving near to me. I got up from the bench and went towards Mike. He saw the movement and drove close to me.

"Thank heaven I found you. Please, let's go home. Please."

I got in the car, feeling like I was the worst person on this earth. We drove home in silence. I went towards the front door, when my husband stopped me.

"Wait." He gently took my hand and opened the door. "Look, you've painted this door. You've made this Christmas wreath and hung it here. To the right of the door hangs a picture of the truck with a prayer for the driver. For me. It wasn't here until you came to this house." We went inside and he said, "You've made this collage devoted to my late mother, father, and your relatives and put it on the wall. Our kitchen, with everything in it, was decorated by you. Our portraits and photographs of the children and grandchildren, and everything else in this house, wherever you look. Your hand touched all of that. Now tell me, how will I live without you here, without all this? I love you so much. I'm trying so hard. I see that you feel bad, but I do not know why. Tell me what I must do to make you feel better Tell me, I'll do it."

There was so much warmth in his words, so much of true love. He sank into a chair with me on his lap, and buried his face in my chest and hugged me gently and firmly.

"I do not know," I whispered, "I do not know." But I felt the terrible pain and sorrow leaving me. Everything started moving into place, it became clear and understandable.

I hadn't lost anything, but only gained. I had my homeland, Ukraine, where I was born and lived for more than half of my life, and where I could go at any time. My children, grandchildren, and friends were waiting for me there. Here, in the United States of America, I had my husband, a man with whom I was going to live my second, better half of life. He was sharing with me his second half of life and all that was in it, I was sharing mine.

Perhaps this is what they call sharing your grief. I guess you must truly love a person to feel him or her that much to be able to take away part of his heart pain, and perhaps even physical pain. I hugged him back and whispered, "Thank you, my dear. I love you too. Forgive me. I don't know why I've felt so bad. But now I know, now I can handle it. Thank you."

The next day I felt sick and weak, though there was no pain, no sorrow anymore. So I decided to stay home. I still felt a little sad, but it was a different kind of sadness, bright and rewarding. God had helped me. Made me wiser. My angel, through Mike, gave me the hint. I was doing everything correctly. I worked hard, loved, missed my family and friends. I dreamt. I realized it was okay to laugh when I felt joyful, to cry when I was sad or hurt. This meant that I was alive. As the singer Vysotsky said, "I breathe, and therefore, I love; I love, and therefore I live!"

I love and therefore I am alive.

———

"Polina, can I have your car? I need to go out," Mike asked.

"Of course. Why do you ask? You always take my car when you needed to."

I wondered why he wanted to take my tiny car. Outside the snow was knee-high, so it was easier to take the pickup. But I forgot about it the second he left, devoting all of myself to cooking dinner.

He returned home in forty-five minutes and sat down at the computer. He didn't say where he went, what for. I didn't ask. After dinner, I went to the garage, not turning the lights on. Suddenly, something alerted me. Something was wrong. I walked over to the light switch and turned it on.

"Oh my goodness!"

Instead of my little Saturn, shimmering with its mother-of-pearl, there was parked a magnificent snow-white car. A Cadillac! I got frozen to the spot, and as soon as I was able to move again I rushed into the room where my husband was sitting in his favorite chair and intently pressing keys on the keyboard, as if nothing had happened.

"Where? Where's my car?" I cried.

Mike beckoned me to come closer. I did, and he put a key in my hand with a warm smile.

"Here is your car."

Chapter Twenty-Nine

S queezing my keys in my hand, I ran outside.

Little soft snowflakes swirled in their winter dance, covering everything in front of the house. It seemed like millions of diamonds were scattered all over the earth by some zillionaire. They were hanging on the bushes, trees, even buildings. Everything was sparkling and shimmering. It wasn't cold, though the thermometer showed minus twenty centigrade. So good. It was all so good! I began to sing.

"It was a winter and first of Christmas Day,
And the whole day we would wander with you.
And all around was solemn and quiet
And white-white snow above white Earth…"

I was singing heartily a famous Soviet song, "Tatiana's Day," and swirling in my own winter dance, imagining myself one of those silver snowflakes.

Snow was slowly falling down on my shoulders, covering my head. Was it winter? That terrible winter with blizzards and frost, white-hair and sickness? There was nothing scary in this winter. Winter could also be very, very nice and warm. Life was continuing. I knew there would be many things in our lives. The important thing was that we did find each other, despite living on different parts of the globe.

"Look, Mike, how beautiful it is all around!" I voiced my thoughts aloud. I had noticed that he was standing in the doorway, not wanting to disturb me. He was standing quietly, smiling, looking at me, and his eyes were so warm and so affectionate.

"Yes, very beautiful. I love winter. Let's go to the cabin and race on snowmobiles, eh?"

"Great! When?"

"When? Well, tomorrow morning!"

And we began to make plans for tomorrow morning, then the next year, then the rest of our lives, which we had decided to spend together. Dreaming, laughing, hugging, kissing. And I realized after winter, spring would come again, followed by summer, autumn. Life went on and was lovely in all seasons.

Snow kept falling and falling, covering the area in front of the house with a sparkling white carpet. I fell into it in the middle of the yard, and began to move my arms and legs, leaving an angel silhouette in the snow. Mike plopped down next to me and did his own angel. Snow was covering our bodies and faces, falling lightly down from heaven, and we kept lying in it, like two snowy angels, looking at the dark sky that rained down on us sparkling white fluff and smiling.